Finding Hollis

Finding Hollis

Pauline Knaeble Williams

PRESS

This book is a work of fiction. The names, characters, places and incidents are products of the writer's imagination or have been used fictitiously and are not to be construed as real. Any resemblance to persons, living or dead, actual events, locales or organizations is entirely coincidental.

Finding Hollis

Design: John Toren

Forty Press, LLC
427 Van Buren Street
Anoka, MN 55303
www.fortypress.com

ISBN 978-1-938473-xx-x

To Bernice Helen Anderson Knaeble.
The story and the characters in Finding Hollis are fictional
but the heart of the book comes straight from my mother.

"Failing to fetch me at first, keep encouraged.
Missing me one place, search another.
I stop somewhere waiting for you."

— Walt Whitman, *Song of Myself*

1

Frances could not recall a colored woman ever riding this line. Most of the black people, and there were not many, lived in small pockets in other parts of the city. She took note of the woman's perfectly ironed dress and, it being a Friday evening, was tempted to assume the woman was off to someplace intriguing. Yet Frances was unable to imagine just where that might be.

The trolley jerked into motion.

The man next to her shifted in his seat, lifting his hat as he ran his fingers through his hair, the scent of pomade growing stronger. She had noticed the mild fragrance when she first boarded the streetcar, how it mixed with the evening air that drifted in through the one open window. Advertisements for shoe polish and chewing gum gleamed above the heads of the many passengers, familiar people she almost knew. On her left, a lady holding a sack of beets hummed quietly and across the way a boy squirmed in his mother's lap, a tuft of blonde hair falling across his forehead. A shaft of sunlight skirted and then held in an unsteady line across the floor, making everything in its slim path shimmer and dance. Frances prided herself on her keen observation of details.

Now as they turned onto Broadway, she looked out at the sidewalks strewn with people bustling between storefronts and parked cars, eager to get home to their evening meal, paying no mind to the passing trolley with its unusual rider, nor to an old pickup truck moving along the avenue. Passing Pearson's Shoe Store, Frances spotted its owner, one knee against the dull hardwood floor, helping a customer.

This was her stop.

She clutched her sweater and got up. She took notice of the sunlight now streaming in honey-like through the front windows then turned her full attention to the back of the car, curious about the woman who had also begun to move toward the door. By the time they reached their mutual destination, Frances found herself standing just behind her.

As she waited, she took in the woman's hair pinned up neatly, her stockings, the sensible black shoes, the matching gray handbag with a pearl-colored latch. But what was most impressive was how firmly her shoulders maintained a line and her neck held her head so gracefully. Frances straightened her own torso, drawing herself up taller, and then allowed her gaze to linger on the woman's skin, the back of her neck and then her arm. A creamy brown color that was really no more than a few shades darker than her own. She studied the woman's gray dress, realizing she had mistaken a pattern of tiny sailboats on a choppy sea for yellow flowers.

The door began to open and the woman reached for the rail. The grace and composure captured in her posture gave way, for a brief moment before Frances's eye, to an underlying sense of uncertainty as her hand, extended in mid-air, trembled. Finally, just as the squeaking sound of the door ceased, she seized the metal rail, leaning into it as she stepped down. When she released her grip, Frances watched the yellow sailboats sink into the street, thinking she had discerned something small but significant about the stranger.

This last thought was shattered by what happened next, for as the woman stepped into the street the truck lurched past the open door. The deep rattle of its motor and the force of its dense, crushing body collided with Frances's neatly stacked perception of the order of things around her. All at once, there was no sense to cuffed pant legs, to filing cabinets, to egg salad sandwiches sliced diagonally, to having one dollar from each paycheck put into war bonds. Everything that she counted on, that defined her day, that kept her on track, was dismantled. There was nothing but the space in front of her where the woman had stood and a million atoms rushing in to fill it.

She gasped as she descended into the street, fleeing after the moving vehicle; the woman's dress caught on the back fender. For a few long moments, the body dragged behind until the truck rounded a corner and the fabric tore away. The vehicle kept going, the victim rolled once, twice. *Things in motion have a tendency to stay in motion*, spun threw Frances's thoughts as she ran faster, panting hard. The woman's body came to an awkward and final stop.

Frances let out a small cry and knelt down. The shoes were gone, the clothes torn, the skin on her bare arms shredded. She lay on her back, her face turned up toward the evening sky. With a trembling hand, Frances laid her sweater over the woman's hip to cover where the dress had frayed. The woman was still alive, her face relatively unmarred and her eyes appeared deep as a well. Frances hovered and then fell into them, losing her balance, her hearing, her sense of time. She stayed there, swimming in the stranger's eyes, for longer than she would ever remember.

Until at last the woman spoke, her voice was clear and firm and her words uttered without repetition. "Find Hollis."

And just like that, her eyes closed. Her forehead, her heart, the top of her smashed thigh eased toward the back of her body, which no longer felt the bite of the pavement. Which no longer felt anything. She did not move again. Slowly, Frances looked up at the circle of people who had gathered. She thought to yell for someone to dial for an ambulance but her voice, dry like a leaf, caught in her throat.

✳

From his shoe shop, Mr. Pearson had heard the truck's muffler as it rumbled alongside the streetcar. There seemed to him a pause; a lapse that was not void of sound, for surely the truck continued to rumble and the whistle of the 5:28 rolled up from the train yard, but a pause that nonetheless made Mr. Pearson stand up and cock his head to the side. Then came the cacophony of cries that drove him to the door. Without taking time to grab his hat, he fled the length of two blocks, weaved through the crowd and bent down next to Frances. He was startled to see before him a dark-skinned woman and then flooded with a sense of impropriety, not only because the torn dress revealed part of her thigh but for the fact that he had never before been in close proximity to a colored woman. Mr. Pearson watched her chest, waiting for it to rise. When it didn't, he considered holding her wrist to try for a pulse, but decided against it.

"Shouldn't we call for help?" Frances asked, finding her voice. She knew the woman was dead but it seemed impossible that there was nothing left to do.

"Yes," Mr. Pearson answered. The closest pay phone hung in a booth up another block and across the street. He had never used it.

"Don't worry," he muttered unconvincingly, staring at Frances's shoulder. "Don't worry."

The small, silver bell attached to the door of Feldman's Jewelry Shop made a delicate sound when Cotton finally pushed himself out into the street.

Cotton had heard the rough engine, the soft squeal of tires at the corner and the accompanying shouts, but hadn't turned from the jewelry case. It sounded to him like trouble, something from which he did his best to stay clear. Behind him, Mr. Feldman made a small noise and then fell silent. This silence, settling like dust on the objects around the room, made Cotton finally turn. He moved to the door, saw a group huddled in the street and yet, did not go out. He could not see Hazel's body on the ground nor did he catch a flash of her dress through the legs of the onlookers, so he told himself it was someone else, that misfortune did not belong to him alone. But he knew better. After the silence had stretched as far as it would go, he left the jewelry shop and strode into the street to claim her.

When he reached Hazel he bent down, feeling the breath of the crowd behind him. In one swift motion he gathered her into his arms and, pulling her in tight, stood up. She was not easy to lift but he welcomed the effort. He had but only a few times, held her so close.

There in the street, next to the sweater that had slipped off as he lifted Hazel, lay a pocketbook. Someone had found it near the streetcar stop and had placed it next to her body. Cotton stared, unable to retrieve it. Frances reached for the gray purse. She extended her arm, then balked; the man's hands were full. She looked to his chest where his shirt was smeared with blood, thinking it could be wedged between them.

"Don't," he whispered. "Don't put anything between us."

Then he turned on his heel and started off, carrying Hazel. He did not get far before a man called to him.

"Sit, Mister. For goodness sake, you must sit," Mr. Schneider pleaded in a thick German tongue that under normal circumstances he worked hard to disguise. He guided Cotton to a set of steps that rose from the sidewalk.

It had been a quiet evening in north Minneapolis, the war on but the Depression over. Now, with the commotion, neighbors gathered on their front porches. Cotton sat, begrudging the people around him. He wanted Hazel all to himself. He wished to call her name, find some part of her still present, but not while they watched. He would not, despite the urging of the trees above him, bow his head toward her chest and weep. Rather he stared at her eyelids. Drove his attention into the smooth soft mounds, trying to get in.

A police car crept up to the curb in front of the Schneider's house. An officer got out slowly, looked at Cotton, then at Schneider, then back at Cotton. His uniform was tucked neatly into his belt but his cap sat slightly askew.

"All right now, all right. We can't have you just sitting here," he paused, looking at Hazel, "on the curb." He contemplated just how far he should step into the situation. "From what I can see, seems too late to go to a hospital. If you can get her in the car, I can drive you where you need to go."

Cotton managed to stand, Hazel still draped in his arms, but as he moved toward the car his strength dropped like the sun behind him. Mr. Schneider opened the door and helped him into the back seat. The policeman was already at the wheel.

"I'm sorry," Mr. Schneider offered, but the car had already pulled away.

✱

Frances stood with one hard, square heel intact and the other lost completely. At what point it had broken off from her shoe, she couldn't say, nor did she wonder. She had watched Cotton—guessing his name to be Hollis—move up the street while her hand grew stiff clutching the pocketbook. After the police car had driven off, Mr. Pearson urged her to go home.

"You're upset," he said, "let your family take care of you."

Mr. Pearson's gaze followed Frances as she left. He did not notice the missing heel despite her limp. His vision was impeded by the disconcerting events that could not be pressed nicely into the corners of the evening. The disparity between sliding an evening slipper on a customer's foot and seeing a woman die, tipped his thinking upside down. And what would nag him, what would follow him up the back stairs to his apartment where his wife and grandson were waiting, after he had darkened the store an hour later, would be the image of the girl's naked thigh and the shame of being unable to dismiss it.

✱

The low angle of the sun spat shadows of leaves onto the pavement all around her as she crept toward home. She too walked up Emerson, as Cotton had, but on the other side of the street. People hovered about, reluctant to return to their dinner, as if some announcement might be made or a bulletin posted giving them the details they desired. But gradually they went back inside, not looking to a young woman, even as she passed at a stricken pace, a stain of blood drying on her crumpled sweater, as someone who might have an answer.

2

Frances awoke early the next morning. She did not get out of bed, thankful it was Saturday, yet neither did she fall back asleep. Battered by her dreams throughout the night, she knew her head would ache if she sat up. She watched the ceiling while her young sister turned, twisting the bedspread. Carol was small but she burrowed her way to the center of the bed each night, tempting Frances to get out one side and back in on the other. This morning she let the child cling to her hip, as she eyed the light fixture on the ceiling, its shape gaining definition as dawn seeped into the room. The shape of the fixture itself suggested an exotic fruit. A guava or maybe a mango, she wasn't certain of the difference.

She considered the mundane and impartial nature of the fixed object on the ceiling. She blinked and once again found herself waiting in front of the open streetcar door, the rattle of the passing pickup loud in her ear. The starched, gray dress with its perfect hemline no further away than an out-stretched hand. She could not shake this part, the second before it was too late. The clear and empty moment that would never come again. It caused her to toss in bed last night and then, when sleep finally arrived, to dream in fragmented circles. With morning coming on, she was again waiting her turn to step from the streetcar into any other evening than the one that had just happened.

She fought the urge to cry.

The familiar sounds of her mother moving about in the kitchen arrived to comfort her. She heard the teakettle filling. She thought she heard the soft ting of a wooden spoon against a pot, as if the Cream of Wheat was already being stirred. There had been money for the gas bill this month so there was no need for her mother to stoke up the left side of the stove with coal. She thought she should get up to help with breakfast, but didn't.

✳

The evening before, she had climbed the front porch as Carol and Howard rushed out to greet her, as they liked to do. They hugged her waist and then Carol reached up on tiptoe to kiss her sister's cheek, but Frances had forgotten to bend down.

"Your shoe, Fran," said Howard excitedly. "Golly, it's gone. The whole back chunk."

"I know Howard."

She kept moving into the house. Her father sat in a chair pulled up under a table lamp fixing the radio. He looked up from his work and into the ashen face of his oldest daughter. Quickly he helped her to the davenport and then called to his wife from the kitchen. Mary came into the room with a dishtowel in her hands, her apron wet with soapsuds. One glance at Frances and her lungs flattened. She sat on the edge of the armchair and leaned forward, panicked to know what had brought her daughter home looking so disheveled.

Through sobs Frances relayed what happened. Her legs shook so much as she spoke so that she had to hold them still with her hands. It was not easy to tell. She left out that she had slowed her pace just slightly to allow the woman to exit the streetcar before her. And she didn't mention anything about being asked to find someone named Hollis. What felt most odd to Frances was that she couldn't find a way to disclose to her family that the woman was colored. It felt like a fact out of place in the telling of the story, although hours earlier it seemed to mean everything.

The pocketbook was still pinned to her ribcage. Her father eased it away and handed it to his wife. The purse held one streetcar token, a tube of lipstick, two Anacin in their small tin and a folded envelope with the words *Feldman's Jewelry, Broadway and Emerson, 6 on Friday* scrawled in pencil. Mary snapped the pocketbook closed, hoping the sound would put an end to the incident for the night. She made her daughter rest on the sofa with her feet up, shoes off, while she went to fix a bowl of soup. She took the stained sweater with her to the kitchen.

∗

Cotton felt the police car lurch to a stop. This time the officer helped him as he struggled to get out.

"Someone needs to come down to the station on Monday. Fill out a report. Otherwise they'll be nothing on file. Understand?"

Cotton thought to nod but didn't. His feet met the pavement as if the cement was wet and meant to hold him down, still he made it up the porch where Lewis Banks stood waiting for his daughter.

They placed her on the sofa. Her mother, down on both knees, pleaded and pleaded for her to wake up until her voice dissolved into a low, steady moan that seemed to tear at the heart of her husband standing tall but utterly wounded behind her. With his eyes he looked into Cotton's for an explanation.

"She was struck by a car, well no, a pickup truck," he began. The words cut against the flesh of his mouth. He tried to continue but what else was there to say? What did it matter, the details, but that she was dead? Yet her parents were waiting for more, so he continued. "She must a just come off the streetcar and then… the truck kept going, didn't stop."

"Why was she…" whispered Lewis Banks, but he couldn't finish his sentence. Hazel was their only child.

Cotton explained why she had taken the streetcar over to Broadway. It was no more than a few miles from where they lived, yet a world they rarely entered. There were stores in their own neighborhood, along Sixth Avenue—including a barbershop, a grocery market, the Chicken Shack—but no jewelry store. Cotton had planned to go downtown for the ring except that while out walking one day he had met an amiable white fellow who insisted he could get a wedding ring for a fair price on Broadway. He had been waiting for Hazel inside the store, studying the small selection of wedding bands that gleamed from under the glass, Feldman eyeing him. Hazel had insisted on picking out the ring, thus, at his suggestion, he had come from work and she had taken the streetcar to meet him at the jewelry shop on the corner of Broadway and Emerson on a mild autumn evening.

The room fell silent. Darkness slipped in, seeping into the despair and disbelief that rolled like fog around their knees. For a moment all three clung to the cover of dusk and the truth it obscured. But they could not stand in the dark forever. When a lamp was turned on the bulb laughed at the foolishness of loving something that could be lost. Cotton dropped into an armchair. He placed his elbows on his knees and rubbed his eyes with the palms of his hands, then abruptly drew up straight in the chair. She was dead, that was all there was, clinging to every last thing that remained. And he hated all that remained. If he dared, he would spit on the rug under his feet, the lampshade, the books on the table beside him, the night air boldly crossing the windowsill, the roses speckled on the papered walls. How dare there be walls that someone would bother to glue paper across. And books with anything worth reading inside. There was nowhere in the room his eyes could land, especially not the sofa.

Contrary to his urge to spit, his mouth was dry as wood. He poured all his energy into his growing sense of thirst and nothing else. His mind clawed at images as they came upon him until they were shredded into nothing more than one pressing need for a sip of water, a need he was determined not to satisfy. He stood to leave. He searched for the smallest thing to say but there was nothing to find. Hazel's mother held him in her arms for a good, long minute. Another twenty seconds and he knew he would have sunk deep into her shoulder, but to his relief and disappointment, she let him go.

He left the house, slipped into a wooded area that backed the homes along the block, and came to a trail that led in one direction to railroad tracks and in the other to a creek. He followed toward the creek. The night was dark and mild, without any hint of the coolness that would soon come to extinguish the last remnants of summer.

As he reached the creek, a sliver of moonlight reflected in its shallow waters. He watched it shimmer and then, as if a fish took it as bait, suddenly disappear into the dark water. Three heartbeats passed before he looked up to see that a small cloud had parked in front of the moon. He found a place to sit among the cattails, and waited. When the reflection returned, he attached his eyes to it as though it might serve as an anchor. But, like everything else, it too knew that she was dead.

Cotton got up and walked back up the path. This time he headed toward the railroad tracks and followed them for hours, until the sky began to lighten in the east. Then he changed directions and headed back.

While the pot of leftover soup warmed on the stove, Frances leaned back against a pillow. Her father rubbed her feet and hummed a tune vaguely familiar to his children as they sat quietly in the room watching each other. Carol was six and crouched at her father's feet with one arm around his leg. Howard, two years older, was also on the floor, pretzel-style, staring at the laces in his father's boots. Raymond, eleven, who had come from outside in the middle of the story and Ethel, just a few weeks short of fifteen, sat on the piano bench.

Frances ate the entire bowl of barley soup and a wedge of bread. At the first spoonful she found she was famished, as if lunch had been a lifetime ago. In fact, everything seemed so long ago. She looked around the room. Hadn't she, at one point, read the magazine now gathering dust under the coffee table? How many years had the piano, with its three dead keys, sat in exactly that spot? Had they not painted the walls once or was that an old hope blurred into a memory? As she hung up her work clothes and put on a housedress, her life before the accident seemed to stretch thinner and thinner toward obsolete.

"A game of checkers?" Ray asked, bringing her back.

She agreed with relief, knowing she needed to occupy the evening in some way. The checkers offered Frances a safe, square place to rest her eyes. Later when it was time to sleep, even when her eyelids closed, it took hours to slow down.

*

When Cotton arrived in his room at the boarding house, after walking most of the night, having passed Miss Emma on the stairs with nothing to offer out of his usual polite and unhurried greeting, he closed the door. He peeled off his blood-soiled shirt and laid stomach-down on the bed. He slept deep and hard just as he had hoped. He awoke to a room dusted with late afternoon light. His throat was parched. He had not taken water since noticing his thirst at the Banks' house. Last night it had served as a distraction and a penance, now it tore at his insides. The glass on the nightstand was empty so he angled down the hallway, bumping against the wall once, until he reached the bathroom. There he drank from cupped hands. The taste of water brought forth a longing so old he felt as if his mother's cheek brushed his ear. He glimpsed the side of her face, a round soft cheek and the half smile of a smile. His mother had died just after his second birthday, leaving him without a memory of her until this moment, a memory that had never surfaced before.

Cotton crumbled to the floor, sobbing into his hands. His body shook, doubly and equally, from the loss of two women he had only begun to love.

Miss Emma, who owned the house, knocked lightly

against the door.

"Baby?" she called. She let herself in, turned the faucet handle off and knelt down on the floor beside him. "Oh, dear sweet child. Ain't nothin' fair. Ain't one damn thing in this whole world fair." This was the first time Cotton had heard a vulgar word pass by Miss Emma's fifty-year-old lips. He brought his head up, regaining some composure.

She looked at his face and let out a sigh.

"Come on now." She helped him to his feet. "Grab a shirt and come on down to the kitchen. You need something to eat. Where you been all night?"

When he got to the kitchen he watched Miss Emma as she vigorously scraped butter onto the toast as if it had misbehaved. She set down a plate in front of Cotton and then moved to the sink to attack the dishes.

He ate silently, worrying that nourishment would make him feel better. He wasn't interested in feeling better. He intended to suffer, the only tangible thing he had left to offer Hazel. He was twenty-six years old and he intended to suffer this day and each day forward.

*

Chayton had lost most of his hearing by nine. One afternoon there was a deer bounding through the woods thirty yards off but no accompanying sound of rustling leaves and snapping branches. The day before he swore he had heard the squirrels in the brush and the birds overhead. Faintly, of course, but heard them enough to pause and look up from the rock where he sat fishing. In truth, his hearing had been fading gradually, but on the day of the silent deer, he realized he could no longer count on the sound of anything. It was worrisome to him and his family; life on a reservation was hard enough without everything turning muffled. He had to learn to adapt, relying on his eyes and his sense of smell and his hands. He continued to fish and hunt for his family, moving within his own silence, the loneliness and the solace of it, noiselessly through the forest tracking a rabbit or a fox or a storm rolling in. He knew what signs to look for; how long ago the animal had rested in the depressed grass, the smell that preceded the smell of rain. But despite his observant and cautious ways, he did not catch everything.

He grew into a young man amidst his family and the others perched along the banks of the Minnesota River, twenty-five miles from the north side of Minneapolis.

On this Friday, Chayton awoke early. He was to drive to Uncle Lee's house, get in a good meal, bargain for a few needed items and then return before nightfall. Uncle Lee had lived for many years in the city where he had chosen to raise his children and grandchildren.

Chayton checked the gas gauge, removed an empty crate from the bed of the truck, and set out, rolling down his window to let in the mild morning. He made it to Uncle Lee's house in time for a breakfast of eggs and fried potatoes. His family greeted him warmly, calling him son and brother. He in return called them father, mother, brothers, as was the way of the Dakota. While he ate they asked after Grandmother and then inquired about the well-being of each person on the reservation, including the young ones they did not know. There were only a handful of children to name, but Chayton was hopeful he would have a few to add some day.

He spent the afternoon, with the help of his cousin, gathering the supplies requested by those back home. Three of the elder women needed fabric, a rusty spade had to be replaced and Lena, who lately seemed to be returning more of his smiles, had mentioned once that she fancied the turquoise-colored beads from the city rather than the oval and rather plain ones from town.

By late afternoon, Chayton had traded a chord of firewood for a used but decent spade from his uncle's neighbor and used one of the dollars to purchase the fabric that the elders would turn into winter clothing. He had sent his cousin, whose skin and hair was light, into the store while he waited outside watching the traffic bump along the busy street. He decided against looking for the beads. Although they would only cost a few pennies, winter was coming and they needed to save whatever they could.

"See you next time, Chay. Drive safe," called the cousin.

But Chayton didn't hear. He was already shifting the gear into forward and turning the wheel. Both headlights were out so he wanted to get home before dark. He pulled off, angling the old pickup along Broadway.

3

Monday arrived. Frances darted across the street and up the steps of a large three-story building the color of sand. She slipped behind her desk and got to work. Her morning sped along, as there was an ample amount of tasks needing her attention. She had the minutes from last week's meeting to type, receipts that were to be filed and, as always, there was the possibility that Mr. Silverman would call her in to transcribe a letter or draft a memo. By the lunch hour, she was hungry as she entered the small cafeteria. She chatted pleasantly with those around her, nibbling on soda crackers and a thick slice of cheese and felt almost certain, as she dabbed at the corners of her mouth with a napkin, that things were already getting back to normal. She figured her fellow workers were aware of the streetcar accident, but only Verle from the switchboard room had actually mentioned it. Everyone else seemed determined to help Frances move past the awful incident by carrying on as if it never happened.

On Tuesday, things went differently. Verle stopped at Frances's desk to pass on a pile of contracts ready for review. Verle had been with the film distribution company, Metro-Goldwyn-Mayer, two years longer than Frances and it showed in her attitude. She breezed about the open floor, stopping to extend a pleasant greeting here and there. She knew all the film brokers by name. She had taken Frances under her wing and each day they shared their coffee break together.

"Hey, gal," Verle chirped. "Hate to give you these but, as they say, that's my job. Although, between you and me, I thought I was hired to take calls, not be a delivery girl. Not that I'm complaining. Any chance I get to move around and see the sights is a-okay with me." She paused, "You feeling okay, honey?"

"I'm fine," replied Frances, mustering a weak smile. She appreciated having a good friend at work but today didn't have the energy that a conversation with Verle demanded. Her mind darted about, searching for an excuse not to break for coffee.

"Gotta get back to the switchboard," Verle said, "the new girl is all on her own. Coffee in ten."

Minutes later, they stood on the pavement outside their building, on the avenue referred to as Film Row, where the women often took their morning break. Verle flashed a cigarette fashionably through her fingers and began to ramble on about what a busy morning she was having, as Frances noticed a line of clouds aiming for the sun.

"What I can't understand," Verle said, "is what that girl was doing in your neighborhood. Not that there's a law saying she *can't* be there, but why? What business could she have had on Broadway? If you ask me, she was probably up to no good. Knowing how they are, I mean."

Frances felt a flush rise up her neck. The rolled up bills hidden in the lipstick case sprang to mind. The morning following the accident she had heard her mother in the kitchen, eased out of bed and crept across the room to find Hazel's pocketbook where it had been placed on top of the piano. She paused before picking it up, then brought it to her nose. It held the smell of pennies. Inside there was a tube of lipstick. It seemed foolish and intrusive, but she had felt compelled to check the shade. She had expected to find a scarlet red, all the rage since the war had started, but was surprised when it was not lipstick at all but two twenty-dollar bills jammed into the small space.

She now looked over at her friend Verle. She took in her thick wavy hair and her well-tailored dress with the soft cashmere sweater hanging from her shoulders. There was never a seam poking through the tops of her sandals or a blouse with a soiled cuff. Verle had earlier that morning offered to lend Frances a pair of shoes to replace the brown, scuffed flats she had been wearing since she lost the heel on her good pair.

"You didn't even see her," Frances said at last.

"You don't always have to have *all* the details. I have that kind of mind, you know. I can piece things together, see. Sniff out what's really going on. Remember that time..." and she launched into a story, one that would have held Frances's attention last week, even perhaps entertained her enough to draw out a chuckle. But today it just bumped against her like an elbow.

The clouds moved over the sun. She shivered. They had another five minutes but she motioned for the door. Verle followed, silenced in mid-sentence.

Later in the cafeteria, which was no more than an extra room with two long tables surrounded by fold-up chairs, a small sink in the corner and a war poster claiming "Loose Lips Sink Ships," she lost her taste for anything sweet. Geraldine Larson was complaining about the insistent mound of housework waiting for her when she got home from work each evening.

"It seems impossible to keep my house in proper order. As it is now I don't get my husband's shirts and trousers ironed but by the morning he needs to wear them."

"Oh sure enough, I've missed polishing the dining table two weeks in a row," added Mrs. Hainsberg with a nervous laugh. "There just never is enough time, is there?"

"Can you believe I still haven't finished those towels? And, you know, now I've forgotten which stitch you told me to use." Others chimed in.

For the first time the conversations around Frances, in which she had always participated, struck her as trite. The debate over the best stitch for hemming a dishtowel seemed almost silly. She stood up. She didn't like thinking of the others in this way. Previously she had enjoyed the rhythm of their lunchtime conversations; polite exchanges rippled with a healthy dose of laughter. She could not guess at the number of beauty tips she had acquired. She had learned that a dab of Dippity-Doo was really the only hope for fine hair, like hers, to hold a pin curl. That vinegar worked extremely well as a hair rinse, not to mention sunburn relief. Geraldine even suggested they send away to Chicago for a ladies' slacks pattern, predicting soon they'd be wearing them to work. At this, the room exploded and Frances remembered joking that next she'd be told that hats were going out of style.

They had been nothing but kind to her and she felt guilty assessing them. She walked to the sink and poured out her soft drink, watching the brown liquid fizzle down the drain. As the bubbles disappeared, popping into nothingness, it occurred to her that the accident had changed her perspective. Everything now seemed a little different, more acute and louder. She had been bothered all morning by the number of chairs around her that groaned and scraped under the weight of shifting people. And she couldn't understand why Verle kept the habit of tapping a red fingernail against her front teeth when reading over a memo.

Even colors. She had never noticed the pink hue in her father's brown cap, the blue pebbles crushed into the stone steps of her office building, or the yellow undertones in her sister Ethel's cheeks. As well, she had never realized how solemn a tree could be. When she had left her house that morning the old elm in the side yard stopped her in her tracks. Had its trunk been so dark and stationary this whole time, despite its swaying branches, its shimmering leaves? Holding so straight for what? she wanted to ask it.

She hurried now, away from the lunchroom. Upon reaching her desk she shoved an unopened chocolate bar into the top drawer and sat down to work. She began typing a letter and then pored over it for errors. It helped to steer her thoughts onto the page in front of her, all the while continuing to yearn for last week when she was just like everyone else. At five o'clock Mr. Silverman called her name. Deep in the fine print on page three of a document, she was startled at the sound of his voice.

"My dear," he said, "you're working much too hard for the end of the day. It will still be here come morning."

Mr. Silverman was her favorite person in the entire office, not because he was the boss but because there was something about him that reminded her of her father, although she hadn't determined just what. It was not his physical attributes. He was a thin man with dark, bushy eyebrows that contrasted wildly with his gray, closely clipped hair, while her father was husky and more weathered than Mr. Silverman. They spoke differently as well. Her boss read books like *Jane Eyre* and talked in sentences she imagined coming out of Mr. Rochester's mouth. She liked to savor his words and imagine rolling them around on her fingertips, feeling their texture. Her father, on the other hand, spoke real regular. And of course, Mr. Silverman was Jewish and her father was, well, just plain American.

"Oh, I must have lost track of the time," she said, a little flustered in his presence, as always.

"Yes, of course," then lowered his voice. "And how are you? I heard about that awful tragedy on the streetcar and the entirely unfortunate outcome for the young lady who perished. How very dreadful for her family and, for you, of course. It will not, I'm certain, be an easy thing to forget, if such a thing is meant to be forgotten."

He paused, looking behind her. The office was buzzing with the activity of the day's end, people straightening the gadgets on their desks, reaching for their coats and hats, checking for their streetcar tokens. "I can see I'm upsetting you, dear. Just know if you need anything, my door is always open." With that he patted her hand and retreated to his own office.

She reached for her coat. The mild weather of last week had turned. She placed a beige hat on her head, angling it by habit to the right, and opened her desk drawer to retrieve her purse and the brown paper bag that was folded up neatly to reuse for tomorrow's lunch. She felt weakened by Mr. Silverman's words and the suggestion that she would not easily forget Hazel, nor perhaps should she. This was the opposite of what most everyone else seemed to be saying and the antithesis of where all her energy had been placed the past four days. She shuffled out of the office and down the stairs, passing the shipping room on the second floor and Warner Brothers on the first. Once outside, she crossed the street and waited in the growing shadow of the city's skyline, along with the other downtown workers and shoppers, for the streetcar to arrive.

In 1944 the Foshay Tower stood as the first skyscraper built west of the Mississippi River. It loomed above office buildings, warehouses humming with activity, and department stores that Frances occasionally visited on her lunch break. Downtown Minneapolis had restaurants like Charlie's and The Nankin, much too fancy for her to go into, but with windows that allowed a peek on a Saturday afternoon when she and Ethel headed down to the Soda Fountain in the basement of Woolworth's. Further east a few blocks sat the warehouse district, where the bars and nightclubs could be found.

Once, years back, she had accompanied her father to the Persian Palms where he delivered a bundle of shirts to the owner. She waited outside with her brother Ray, mindful of how fast dusk was coming. From where they stood, she could see the heavy limestone of the Foshay Tower stretching upward, its long antenna fading into the deepening sky. In school they had learned that the Tower was built to resemble the Washington Monument. Inside, the rooms had floors lined with imported marble and banisters made from African Mahogany. It was said the ceilings were laced with silver and gold, and to open the doors one had to turn gold-plated knobs. Everyone knew the story of how Mr. Foshay had lost his fortune just months after the building was completed. First the market crashed and then later a trial uncovered shady business deals. Even so, no one could deny the building's beauty and Frances had been eager for the school fieldtrip when she finally got inside to see the three commissioned busts of George Washington.

The door to the Persian Palms opened suddenly. She squeezed Ray's hand. Out first, barged a burly man whose voice shot into the coming night, "Left the little nippers on the step, eh Walt?" From behind the man stepped Walter, grinning at his children. With one arm he turned them around, raised a hand in parting, and off they went. As they walked up Washington Avenue, which ran parallel to the river, and past the train station, Frances marveled at how many men dressed in tatters greeted her father by name.

She now bristled as the streetcar pulled up. Yesterday, at this juncture, she had kept her apprehension at bay. But as she approached the open door on Tuesday, dread rushed to the pit of her belly and stomped its foot. She froze. There was no direction in which her limbs would agree to move. She felt a strong need to stop and think but instead the crowd swept her up the steps and into the car. She landed clumsily in a seat and closed her eyes against the abrupt motion. She focused on counting the seven stops that brought her to her corner on Broadway. Opening her eyes, she let the crowd flush her back out. When she surfaced she was staring at herself in the window of the darkened storefront of Stanley's Furniture Store, which hadn't been open regularly since Stanley's son had died in the war.

For a moment, her reflection didn't register. She saw

someone older, wiser but also worn, that she would have passed on the street and from whom she would not have received a greeting. It was her eyes that peered out differently and then, even as the other features came forward in a familiar rush, the eyes remained remote, like two guests at a party that didn't know anyone else. The eyes were no longer lashes around two blue marbles, content to merely settle for and then reflect the pleasant surface of complex things.

"Hi-ya Frances!"

She jumped. Then turned to find the wide, ruddy face of Joe Mallory grinning at her. She had watched Joe at church only two Sundays ago and been startled by the sudden desire, though she had known him since second grade, to see him barefoot. Feet, particularly toes, were so personal she had felt immediately embarrassed to be contemplating Joe Mallory's instep during Hymn number 212.

"Hello," she managed.

"How's things?" Everyone knew he had a bum knee from a football collision so didn't need to ask why he wasn't enlisted.

She shrugged, feeling almost nauseous.

"I saw you at Mass on Sunday in that pretty yellow dress," he said.

"The yellow dress?" she asked.

"You looked nice."

"The yellow dress? The one with the worn elbows that I have to keep a sweater over to hide? The one I would give to the ragman if he still came around with his horse and wagon?" She let out a weird laugh. "The one I would mop up the floor with if the roof leaked?"

"Heck, you and yellow are a good pair, that's all I mean to say."

She just stared at him while he shrugged his shoulders.

"Sorry Joe, I'm being rude. It's just that the color yellow strikes me as odd today. I'm on my way home now."

"Sure thing," he said, stepping backward. He smiled a

little and she softened against it.

When he was gone she began to cry, just a quiet roll down each cheek as she moved on. A whole day of emotion had aligned behind her brow until there wasn't anywhere else for it to go. Tonight the street was quiet, the clouds bringing on a false dusk and the temperature too cool for porches. She walked, shoulders down, with tears spilling along her face, hoping no one was watching.

✳

Mrs. Schneider was at her window. She stepped around the dining room table, where she had been arranging towels into tall clean stacks, when she saw Frances moving up the street. From behind lace curtains she was unable to detect actual tears, but thought the girl's face seemed as soft as a brown paper bag. Mrs. Schneider felt a surge of empathy, quickly matched by anxiety as she recalled what happened after her husband had led that poor Negro man to their steps.

Unlike her husband, Mrs. Schneider had been born in America. Her great-grandparents had come from Germany a hundred years back. While she could still manage a sauerkraut dinner she was undisputedly American enough, like most of her neighbors, to be removed from any connection with the Nazis. For her husband, on the other hand, the distinction was not so clear.

Four days before, soon after the police car had turned the corner taking Cotton back to the other side of town, Ralph from next door and two other men from down the block, angled over to the Schneider's front lawn. Mrs. Schneider didn't hear most of the conversation because of the stew she was tending to on the stove, but she did catch the end.

"Well that's good of you to help a man in need, Heinrich," Ralph was saying, "but a nigger is a nigger and I wouldn't have placed a hand on that boy if you'd paid me a silver dollar."

One of the other men nodded and slapped Ralph on the back.

Ralph continued, "But now see, you're not from around here, so you might not be all clear on who's the good guys and who ain't." Ralph was heading for a topic that terrified Mrs. Schneider. She would not let her husband, just because of a slight accent, be aligned with Germany. He hadn't lived there in twenty years.

She came out the front door in a hurry.

"Oh Ralph, good evening," she said trying to sound surprised to find him there. "How's Leona? She must have one of her delicious suppers on the table? It is that hour you know and, excuse us, but the table is set. Good night then, gentleman?"

She hooked her arm in her husband's and guided him up the porch steps. Inside she squeezed her forehead with one hand.

"Why don't you tell him your name is not Heinrich?"

"I cannot teach him my name," Henry Schneider answered, "if he does not want to learn it."

Her misdirected anger eased. She was calmed by her husband's ability to be insightful amidst insult. She kissed the top of his head as he sat down at the table. The stew bubbled on the stove, the potatoes not yet tender.

Frances now disappeared from Mrs. Schneider's view as she rounded the corner and moved behind a neighbor's hedge. She had but one block before she reached her family's house, with its peeling coat of paint and slanted porch. As she approached, her gaze returned to the elm tree. There it was, exactly as she left it. The trunk broad and wet-gray, claiming its position just as confidently now in the hushed light, as it had in the morning. As she passed and made her way up onto the porch she heard the leaves in the branches rustle. In that rustling she heard a distinct tap against the drums of her ears. "Find Hollis," it beat.

Slowly she turned back toward the tree and to the evening

that now settled in the green lilac bush near the shed and eased along the steep roof of a neighboring house. The light from the kitchen window across the way had begun to reach daringly through the pane.

"I did," she whispered, distraught.

4

Cotton rummaged through the drawer of the nightstand in his room. He found a pencil and a slip of paper. It was Sunday morning, two days since he had lost Hazel. He was waiting for Miss Emma to go off to church, then he'd leave her a note. His hand shook as he drew the pencil toward the paper. The night before he had been plagued by an urge to flee, to follow the train tracks west. But he had not. His body had been so wracked with exhaustion that he eased back on the bed and fell into sleep. For most of his life, he had sacrificed rest for work, had pushed himself relentlessly toward a better life. With Hazel gone, there was nothing ahead and his body knew it. Come morning he forced himself out of bed. He had packed his bag, he just needed to write the note.

He closed his eyes and there was Hazel. Not with the cold and lifeless face of the woman he carried home just days before, but the real one. The one out of which brilliant eyes flashed, the one with so much to say. The face that seemed to glow the first time she answered the door on the bitterly cold day he found her, eight months earlier.

It was a January morning when he arrived in Minneapolis. He stood on the train station platform with nothing but a duffel bag and a rattling heart, pulling down his cap and turning up the collar of his coat.

On his journey from Arkansas, he had traveled more miles by foot than he could reasonably claim, interspersed with a handful of hitched rides that dropped him off in other cities he did not consider his final destination. He was bound for the state which claimed the headwaters of his wide, winding river, the Mississippi. In the end, with winter biting deep into his skin, he indulged in a train ticket.

He now debated which way to go, knowing absolutely nothing about the city of Minneapolis or where he might find a place to stay. It occurred to him that he had been harboring the vague illusion that there would be someone waiting for him or, at the very least, a sign acknowledging he had made it to the right place. But there were no YMCA letters on the building across the street, no hotel announcing vacancies.

He glanced left and then right. Washington Avenue was a mess of snow mounds, with barely a moving vehicle as pedestrians trudged through a morning of heavy snowfall. There was not a sign, visible or imaginary, welcoming him. He felt his enthusiasm dim. He again looked left and again right. Then a porter, just finishing a six-day shift, trudged past with a small bundle of his own tucked under one arm. His wool cap pulled over his graying hair to protect his ears.

"Excuse me, sir," Cotton shouted into the wind.

The man stopped. The snow struck his face. He didn't wait for Cotton to speak but offered loudly, "If you need some place to stay follow behind me. Keep close and step into my footprints. Let my back shield you. I'll hear if you fall too far behind. You got three miles in you?"

Cotton nodded vigorously and then swallowed hard. He had worried that northerners would be standoffish but the porter hadn't even blinked at the sight of a young man, underdressed and disorientated.

The porter had been working this train from Minneapolis to Milwaukee to Chicago and back for years. Since the war started he had witnessed the millions of southerners streaming northward toward opportunity. Most of them headed for the big cities east of Minnesota but it wasn't surprising to see a young man daring to stretch a little further west. During the ride, he had watched Cotton discretely, but almost compulsively, trying to dismiss the weight of a premonition.

They pushed through downtown, passing Film Row where the sidewalks that had been shoveled thirty minutes earlier were already an inch deep again. When they turned northwest and began moving up Glenwood Avenue, the snow came at them head on and seemed to be laced with an icy sting. Cotton kept his head down and concentrated on the footprints of the man ahead of him, knowing he was not getting the worst of it but struggling anyway. Further out they crossed over to Sixth Avenue and after another mile and a few turns, they wound along a street that backed against a creek. Because the snow had softened or perhaps only the angle at which they walked had changed, he was able to look up at the houses around him. The sadder ones without paint, reminded him of home. The man in front began to slow and Cotton knew they were approaching their destination.

It was a small stretch, less than a half square mile in all, where the black folks on this side of downtown were relegated. The porter and his wife had owned their home since before the Depression. They would have lost it in the 30's, when the unemployment rate soared and it seemed like everyone they knew was on relief, except that Lewis Banks was lucky enough to keep his job as a Pullman Porter for the Great Northern Railroad. As modest as the house was, the Bank's made sure that it shined. There was not a fleck of chipped paint or a warped board that hadn't been repaired. Had they not been so warm and generous, giving regularly from their abundant Victory Garden during the warm months, the neighbors may have seen fit to resent such a blatant reminder of the erratic nature of where good and less-than-good fortune falls.

A thick wreath, adorned with pinecones and the orange berries from the Mountain Ash growing in the back yard, hung on the front door. As the men ascended the steps, Cotton stomped his soaked leather boots against the boards of the porch. He heard the door open. There stood Hazel, lit from behind by soft golden light that Cotton mistook, momentarily, for steam. She looked so warm and welcoming that he caught himself leaning forward.

"Father," she sang, "get in here before you catch your death." Then to Cotton's delight she looked over at him before pulling her father into the house.

The men stepped inside, pried off their coats and boots, and looked up to find Mrs. Banks had come from the back of the house where the aroma of a hot meal threatened to overtake Cotton's clear thinking. Hazel stood quietly nearby.

"You must be frozen through. Like a block of ice on a Monday," said Mrs. Banks to Cotton, not waiting to find out who he was but immediately reaching to help him. "With nothing but a flannel shirt under that thing you certainly can't call a winter coat. You can't get by around here dressed like that unless you fancy pneumonia."

"Camille," Mr. Banks interrupted, "we all know you'd wrap a shawl around a bear in the middle of July from worry it might catch a sniffle. There'll be plenty of time for fussing after we get these wet things off."

"I have forgotten my manners, haven't I Lewis?" she rebounded. She threw her husband a penetrating smile, as he had yet to introduce the man she was threatening to wrap a shawl around, speaking of manners.

Lewis Banks explained, "I shared a train ride with this young man. Where did you say you came up from, son?"

"Arkansas, sir, 'bout where it hugs up on Tennessee."

Turning toward Mrs. Banks he continued, his voice choppy in his cold throat, his stomach rumbling. "My name is Cotton Lockhart. My birth certificate says something else but seems 'bout forever since they just called me Cotton."

"Well, Cotton I'm pleased to meet you, and this is our daughter Hazel. You come sit around the kitchen stove and dry out. I'll fix you a plate of food."

"Yes, ma'am. Thank you."

Not daring a glance at Hazel, he followed Mrs. Banks into the kitchen. Yellow paint brightened the walls, curtains hung from the window over the sink. The pot lids on the stove jingled from the food bubbling beneath. The dreary day outside made the room glow from within. This is why he'd come. He knew it, holding the room tenderly in his gaze. This is what he wanted.

After finishing a full helping of smothered pork chops, buttermilk biscuits and green beans picked at the end of last summer and canned specifically for winter days when Lewis Banks came home from a long stretch of work, Cotton was still shivering. Hazel, perched behind him on a step-stool and pretending to read, noticed and pointed so her mother would see his torso shake involuntarily every fifteen seconds or so.

Camille Banks filled the teakettle with water and set it on the stove to heat. The water from the faucet poured only cold, and despite long-range plans to purchase a hot water tank, for now it took an hour of hard labor to draw a bath. She did the same with two other large kettles.

"What brings you to Minnesota, Cotton?" Lewis asked. "You got family here or a job lined up? This is a cold place to land just by chance."

Cotton hesitated. How could he explain his choice without sounding impetuous? How could he explain that the hard decision was to leave, not where to end up?

"I heard about the race riots in Detroit last summer, and found Chicago too noisy," he offered at last. "So I came up this away. I don't have any family but my daddy back home. I used to live just a few miles from the river, the same one comes through here. I was wondering how close is it?"

"Fact is, it's not so far, but don't make plans to set out on a day like this to see it," said Camille just as the teakettle began its whistle.

This brought a smile to Cotton's face, a smile that gave Lewis the same strange feeling of foresight that he had on the train. It made him look over at his daughter. But she had missed it, head bent over the same blurry line in her book.

"After your coat dries," Lewis instructed, "I'll show you where Miss Emma lives. You can see the house out the front window. She takes borders and might not make you pay up front if you can promise it to her soon enough. Which means you need to find a job first thing. You're lucky jobs ain't so tight anymore. What kinda work can you do?"

"Well I can work a field better than most but I reckon that won't do much for me this time a year," he answered, noticing the slight urgency in Lewis's voice that hadn't been there before. "I can read and write. And I can cut through the vocab page of Reader's Digest like butter, not that that guarantees a proper sentence."

Camille turned from the stove and took another look at Cotton. Hazel's head came out of her book. Lewis seemed to soften again.

"Son, that's a good thing, reading and writing. You have pleased the schoolteacher over there and her daughter, the bookworm, but you might need to rely on your more handy skills. Just to get you going. The Ordnance Plant is real good about hiring us folks and I'd imagine the guys staying over at Miss Emma's will know if the meat-packers are still looking for men."

Cotton nodded, he was glad he had not—despite a momentary urge—mentioned his impractical and secret love of drawing. Camille lifted the teakettle to bring up the narrow flight of stairs. She always saved the heavier pots for her husband to carry.

Lewis looked over at her and then hopped to his feet. "Ready then? Hazel, please find Cotton's coat. We better hurry before Miss Emma fills up her last room."

Camille set the teapot back to the stove. She knew there were at least two rooms that had been open for weeks. She also knew Miss Emma had saved up for a hot water tank and could offer her roomers a weekly bath without the backache, or the puddles up the staircase.

Cotton stood up stiffly, thanking Mrs. Banks repeatedly for the nice meal.

"When Mr. Banks gets home from riding I like to cook up something special." She reached out to offer Cotton a slice of pecan pie set on a small white plate. Standing so close to him, she noticed how weary he looked. His clothes were dirty and worn, his hair asking for a cut. She considered persuading her husband to let him stay until he was warm and clean, but then Hazel arrived with his coat.

He nodded before taking the coat out of her hands. Then he set the plate of uneaten pie on the table.

"I sure hope one day I'll get the chance to enjoy one of your pies proper, Mrs. Banks," he said, looking mostly at Hazel.

✳

Within a week he had found a job. He had considered heading to the outskirts of the city to work at the munitions' plant but then heard of a warehouse by the river that needed men to unload shipments of lumber. Wanting to be near the river where he could take his lunch break, he had proven to the supervisor, halfway through the first day, that it had not been a mistake to hire the company's second black man.

He had also, within a week, won the favor of Miss Emma, enjoying her kitchen almost as much as he relished his brief visit to the Banks' yellow one. And he fell asleep each night wondering which bedroom window belonged to Hazel. Then one icy Saturday morning, walking head down as he cautiously chose his route up the block to the boarding house, he heard her call. Had he known how treacherous a simple walk could be he would have opted to spend the morning in his room. But the cold appealed to him, along with city life that he had been waiting for years to explore. Layered in clothes Miss Emma had saved from a former border, he gave

in regularly to the urge to be outdoors. Yet he did not appreciate this morning's challenge of ice-slicked sidewalks.

"Cotton!" Hazel's voice rang out into the quiet, stiff morning. She was bundled in a long coat and what looked to be
her father's wool hat, standing still on the sidewalk twenty
yards away.

As he looked up, he lost his footing and his legs flew out
from under him. He landed hard on his hip. When she ran
over to him, he winced in pain and embarrassment. He rose
slowly, expecting at any moment that his feet would abandon
him again. She reached out and grabbed his arm. Through her
glove, his wool coat and three shirts, he could feel the warmth
of her hand.

"Well, no wonder, look at your boots," she said. "They
may work fine on a dusty road in Arkansas but those fellows
have no business in snow and ice. You need some rubber overshoes to dare a sidewalk like this."

He smiled at her. He couldn't help it. The sooner she knew
the better. He was not oblivious to the effect his smile had on
people, which is why he had spent most of his life working to
diffuse it. But in a new town he was a new person and there
was no reason now to stay withdrawn. He sent all he had in
her direction, letting it slide across his face.

She didn't budge.

"Yep, what you need is a good pair of overshoes. You don't
study that in a book, now do you? That lesson takes a good
hard fall to learn. You're not hurt are you?" She had released
her grasp on his arm.

"Miss Banks, if I can make it down this block without
another spill I will ignore, out of gratitude, any bone I done
broke thus far."

She giggled, "Hmmm, I must admit, I do like how you
mix up all those words that must have come from books with
all those that came just from living. If I may ask, what sub-
jects have you studied?"

"Studied? You make it sound like I attended a fancy college," he smiled. "It was nothing more than me and my daddy sitting around after sundown, reading a little. Out of all those books, the illustrations are what intrigued me most. I reckon I never realized how complicated the human heart was until I tried to draw it. Or how intricate a butterfly was until I had to sketch two symmetrical wings."

He noticed how she tilted her head, as she looked hard at him. What was it that made her eyes shine, he wondered? In the moments that elapsed before she spoke, he realized that even if it wasn't the smile that worked, something had.

"If it's not too much on your manhood I could lend you my arm to get you over to Miss Emma's," she said finally.

"No, not too much at all."

By the time they had shuffled to the front steps of the boarding house, his left biceps, which she had wrapped her entire arm around to keep him in prone position, seemed to smolder from her touch. As she released her grasp, he turned to face her. Even her cheeks held a warmth he desired to touch.

He said softly, "Given I get me a pair of these shoe-overs, Miss Hazel Banks, would you consider joining me next time I go out walking?"

Her mouth opened, closed, opened again. Then, "Overshoes, it is, not shoe-overs but overshoes." Another pause until, "Yes, I suppose I could walk with you, Mr. Lockhart."

He didn't plan what happened next, did not indulge in a speck of contemplation. This was the new him, after all, in his new life. He just went with the urge, leaned over and kissed her. The kiss would have landed solid on the cheek except she saw it coming and turned her head to make it glance off the ear. She stepped back, her eyes ablaze as she looked up at the windows behind them and then quickly down the block at her own house.

"How dare you be so fresh? I haven't been on a proper date yet with you. Or anyone else for that matter. I can't be seen kissing on the front steps in broad daylight. I'm the daughter of a former schoolteacher and my father is a proud member of the Brotherhood of Sleeping Car Porters. You can't just kiss me. Without even asking."

"You're right. I apologize. I don't know what got in to me. That was, well..." and he paused. "Might you a said yes if I'd asked?"

"I did say yes. I said yes, I would go on that walk with you, granted you're not slipping around like a fool trying to take me down with you. I said yes. Now when should I expect you?" She drew her fingers, inadvertently, to her ear.

He noticed and smiled slowly.

∗

Cotton opened his eyes and shook his head. He was supposed to be writing a good-bye note to Miss Emma. He scribbled her name on the paper but could think of nothing further to say. He drew the petal of a daisy and then another until he had drawn a small bouquet in place of an explanation. He left it on the nightstand, crossed the room and grabbed his duffle bag from where it sat under the window. He glanced out, his eye drawn by a figure moving up the street. Astonished, he realized it was the white fellow who had told him about the jewelry shop. He watched the man continue down the block and climb the steps of the Banks' house, Hazel's pocketbook clutched in one hand.

5

Hazel Banks had spent Friday morning, her last morning, helping her mother sort books. Lewis had brought four heavy boxes down from the attic and placed them in the center of an empty bedroom on the second floor. There were far too many books to consider adding them to the bookshelf in the living room, so the women decided to turn the small extra bedroom into a library. Hazel had been urging her mother to bring the books down for a long time, not realizing that sealed up in the boxes was a dose of bitterness that Camille had been storing for years.

Softened by her daughter's recent and contagious surge of cheerfulness, Camille had finally agreed to let Cotton bring over a handful of planks of wood, which took only an afternoon to convert into bookshelves. Preparing the room turned out to be more enjoyable than she could have predicted as mother and daughter, over the course of a week, spent their free time together scrubbing and sewing and then hanging new curtains for the room.

On Friday morning while the women prepared to open the first box, Lewis was in the backyard tending to his mustard greens. Cotton was at the river, waiting for a truck to back up to the loading dock. Frances was downtown at her desk enjoying a slow morning as she practiced her signature on a piece of scratch paper, determined to turn her F from flowery to refined. And Miss Emma, just down the block from the Banks, was pinning sheets and pillowcases rinsed in lemon water to the line in her backyard. While they worked, the mailman slowly made his way up the block.

"What is it mother?" Hazel asked. Camille had bent back the flap of a box and paused.

"Nothing," she insisted and reached quickly in to pull out a tattered fourth grade reader. "It's just been ages since all of this."

✳

Back in West Virginia, Camille had grown up determined to become a schoolteacher. Being bright and well spoken, it was a smooth transition from student to teacher. Her community, small but noteworthy, praised her often over the fine work she did with the children. She, as well as the others, had high expectations. After all, they lived in the very neighborhood in which Booker T. Washington had grown up; attended the very school, it was said, that he had thirty years earlier. Few knew or remembered that Booker T. had spent very few days in the schoolhouse. Working as a salt packer by age nine had kept him from the education he so desperately craved and only later would begin to attain as a houseboy for the owner of the coal mine, learning to read and write from the mistress of the house.

Two generations later, Camille had been teaching for twelve years in the segregated school, using her enthusiasm and diligence to make up for the lack of supplies. She strove to impart upon the children any ounce of knowledge they were willing to absorb. And then a not-so-small miracle happened. Although it had been ten years into her marriage to Lewis Banks, she suddenly dreamt of holding a baby girl. She had the same dream twice over before she noticed that the taste of tomatoes repulsed her and that she had trouble catching her breath when climbing the hill to the schoolhouse. They named the baby Hazel.

A year later, Lewis convinced her to move to Minnesota. He wanted to leave, in part, to flee from the strife caused by the coal mine wars between union organizers and mine owners that had tainted their town, but mostly with the hope that he might land a job with the railroad. When they arrived they had nowhere to go but to where most people arriving in a new city went, a settlement house. They found the Phyllis Wheatley House in north Minneapolis. They were given a small room of their own to get them through a bitter winter while Lewis looked for work. The endlessly long season and the small community of black people, even compared to their home state, required an adjustment for Camille. Where was everyone? she wanted to ask. And she could predict, without needing to inquire, the difficulty in finding a teaching position. Her only hope was to be hired at one of the few schools filled with a significant number of black students. She found, even here, it was assumed that a white teacher would be more effective.

In place of a steady teaching job, she helped out with every program she could at the Phyllis Wheatley House, a center that offered an array of services to new arrivals but also to those more settled into the community. During the Depression, she led a training course for nursery school teachers and taught classes on Negro history and culture, subject matter she considered pertinent especially when infused with lessons of literature and composition. Unfortunately, these intermittent opportunities of being in a classroom setting did not satiate her ambition. She ended up leaving much of her love for teaching in the four boxes of books that stayed under a window in the attic. The part she kept out she poured onto her child who in turn was bright, well-spoken and equally enamored by the idea of becoming a teacher. Camille justified the storing away of needed books by telling herself that one day Hazel would put them to good use.

"Musty," Hazel said bringing a book to her nose. "They need a good airing out. I'll open the windows and we can spread the books out on the floor."

"That'd be fine," Camille said quietly, "'I've got to get to my ironing." The smell and even the hard edges of the books themselves seemed to lean uncomfortably against the place in her chest reserved for her heart.

"Mother, don't you want to look at these?" Hazel implored as Camille headed out of the room. "Half are not even children's books. Why, I could have been reading these all along." She looked up to find her mother already gone. She returned her gaze to the book in her hand, *Incidents in the Life of a Slave Girl written by Herself* (Harriet A. Jacobs). Hazel studied a photo dated 1894 of the author and then opened to the chapter entitled "The Lover." It began "Why does the slave ever love? Why allow the tendrils of the heart to twine around objects which may at any moment be wrenched away by the hand of violence?"

Meanwhile in the kitchen Camille stood at the ironing board waiting for the iron on the stove to heat, the lines across her forehead deeply drawn. Soon after they arrived in Minnesota and she realized there would be no teaching position, she found Royal Laundry on Plymouth Avenue needed women to iron tablecloths and napkins. She spent a good portion of each morning starching, pressing and folding the white linen into neat bundles she then secured with twine. In the beginning Lewis had attempted to carry the laundry in a sack that he dropped off on his way to the station, but soon found he couldn't keep up with the amount she produced. So the laundry mat, pleased with her precise and consistent work, now had their truck, out on Mondays and Fridays, swing by to pick up the bound bundles and leave a wrinkled batch in their place. She sighed now as she lowered the hot iron to the fabric. The truck would be here by noon and she had a pile left to get through.

In the hallway, through the mailbox slot attached to the front door, a letter addressed to Hazel Banks slid through the opening and landed face down on the floor. Hazel heard it, heard the swish of the envelope brush against the hardwood floor. The sound traveled up the staircase and into the room where she sat cross-legged with the book in her lap. The sound kissed her on the cheek so that she looked up and imagined the letter waiting for her below. Careful to keep her page, she placed the open book face down on the rug and rose to her feet. She would come back for the book a few hours later, slide something between the pages and then return it to the floor. The book would stay like that, in that spot with a letter tucked inside it, for the next three months.

Normally she paid little attention to what the postman dropped through the mail slot. On mornings when she noticed letters sprawled on the floor, she would stop to pick them up and set them on the side table without a second look. Today she reached for the one solitary letter, turned it over and found her name on it. Puzzled she walked out to the front porch and eased herself onto the swing. With one finger poised under the flap of the envelope, she looked out toward the yard where she spotted the first yellowing leaves in the maple tree, wondering who would send her a letter. The breeze was mild as it lightly lifted the collar on her dress.

For a moment, she let her attention wander toward the upcoming school year in which she would be volunteering her afternoons at Sumner Elementary School. She had made it clear to the principal, who knew her from her days as a student, that one day she hoped for a class of her own. He had patted her arm and told her helping out the other teachers was nothing short of admirable. She did not find much assurance in his response, nonetheless she now felt a burst of excitement thinking of how it would all begin on Monday.

With a start she realized Miss Emma was waving to her from down the way. She raised her arm to respond only to find the letter still in her hand. She opened it quickly. It began: *Dear Hazel Banks, There is something about me and Cotton you best know....*

The horn of the laundry truck sounded even before the truck had rolled to a stop in front of the house. She dropped the letter, reached down to retrieve it and then had to slide it under the swing's cushion as her mother came out on the porch.

"He's early," Camille complained, then shouted with forced courtesy to the white man, "Be right out, sir. Just gathering it up." The man stared straight ahead and chewed a toothpick. She darted back in the house to call her husband to come collect the bundles; she didn't like to bring them out to the man herself. Lewis was washing his hands at the sink so the dirt from the garden wouldn't soil the linen.

"He's early, isn't he?" he asked, craning his neck to see the clock on the wall.

"At least I finished," she said handing him the first of the bundles. "Hurry on out now, you know how he gets." She frowned at herself for rushing him toward the door, as if her husband, a Pullman Porter, should feel obligated to appease a laundry truck driver.

Hazel was still on the porch swing with the letter hidden under her. It would be until mid-afternoon when her father was back in the garden and her mother in the kitchen, before she could return to the letter and discover its contents. After reading it she sat stunned, then forced herself upstairs where she perched on the edge of the bed for another stretch, staring out the window. She attempted to deflect the impact of the letter by busying herself with preparations; freshening up with a damp cloth, powdering her skin and retying her hair. She put on a gray dress with yellow sailboats and reached for the lipstick tube. A week earlier, her mother had rolled the bills up and smiled as she showed Hazel how to fit them into the small space.

"My mother did the same for me," Camille had said and held up the ring on her finger. "Think of it as a family tradition. The difficult part is finding a way to give the money to Cotton without hurting his pride."

While Hazel appreciated and accepted her mother's

generosity she really wanted everything else about the ring to be between her and Cotton. So, according to plan, she told her parents she had been invited to dinner on Friday evening by a girlfriend. Before leaving the house she wrote on the now empty envelope—the letter tucked safely within a book—the address to the jewelry store and the time of the meeting. She knew this information by heart, but gained a degree of comfort having it down on paper. Feeling shaky, she didn't trust the numbers to float around in her head amidst so many strong, flashing thoughts. She put the envelope, along with the lipstick tube, in her gray pocketbook and let out a disheartened sigh.

Because she was deceiving her parents—planning to walk past her friend's house and keep on toward the street-car stop—and because the content of the letter now left her needing to clutch to something certain, she reached for a hug from each of them for her last good-bye.

Chayton edged the truck into the spot where he always left it and cut the engine. A noise rattled around under the hood for a while before going quiet. He got out. The sun had set, so as he lifted the spade from the back and carried it to the shed beside the house, he was careful of his step in the half-light. He wrestled to close the shed door, pushing it with his hip, then looked up at the house where he knew his grand-mother waited. But he turned away, heading into the woods. After a visit to the city, he needed to go back under the trees where he belonged. The leaves danced above, tickled by the wind. He watched for a while and then walked further on, his step more sure here in the woods where he knew the earth by heart, rather than back in the yard among objects other people could leave lying around.

His grandmother would see the truck and know he was back; know where he had gone and why. She was like him, needed to be under the sky and near the water. After a spell he turned back, arriving at the house with the night gone dark, save the scattering of a million stars and one, lone lamp shining from the window.

The next morning Grandmother had her walking stick and was waiting outside the door when he awoke. He nodded at the sun just flickering through the trunks of trees. "Sleepyhead," she said. There was a can of dirt and worms at her feet.

They walked slowly toward the river, taking a narrow but well-worn route. She went in front so he could see that her steps were steady. She stopped now and then, turning her head. He knew she was listening for something, something he would never hear. He liked to see her ear turned up like that to the birds, the other ear down to what crawled along the ground.

After traveling near a mile, she drew still, then pointed with her cane at a stand of trees and saplings clumped together. From her pocket she took out a kitchen cloth and handed it to Chayton. She waved the stick again to indicate that there was something beyond the trees. "Breakfast," she mouthed.

Chayton found the elderberry bushes and plucked off the purplish-black berries, placing them into the worn, clean cloth. His back was to a small meadow and the early sun found him while he worked. The weather could turn anytime, he knew, so he enjoyed the warmth of the moment. He understood this was the time of year the berries ripened but he had not known that a cluster of the bushes hid in this spot. He would return tomorrow with a pail so that he could gather enough for jam.

When he had made his way back to Grandmother she was perched upon a hollowed log, resting. He joined her, holding the cloth open between them so that they could eat the tart berries while they watched the day grow strong.

6

Hazel found her way into Frances's dreams on Tuesday night, the same night Frances had walked home from the streetcar stop, weeping past Mrs. Schneider's window and pausing briefly under the elm to hear it whisper.

She had entered a house full of noise, Carol and Howard banging away at the piano keys with Ray shadowboxing around them in circles. They didn't notice her as she stood just inside the room taking off her coat. She sighed, relieved by the familiar sounds and sights of home. Her mother appeared from the kitchen and clapped her hands twice to gain attention. The room swirled to a stop.

"Frances!" Carol cried, the first one to spot her, and ran to kiss her cheek.

"Oh," said Mary. "I didn't hear you come in. You look like the wreck of the Hesperus. Are you ill?"

"No, I'm absolutely fine," she assured, kissing Carol's cheek in return. "It smells good in here. Do you need help with dinner?"

"I need help with a song," Mary piped, enthusiastically matching the upbeat tempo of her daughter's voice. She sat down on the piano bench and began to play, making a substitute hum for the three dead keys. Frances joined the singing.

By the song's end, the surge of good cheer she had captured on her homecoming began to fade. In her elbows and knees settled the heaviness of her thoughts, so that she came to envy her mother's place at the piano bench. At dinner she leaned into her chair and offered only a nod or smile to the conversation. She used a book until bedtime to find solitude.

She quickly fell into sleep, landing in a humid dream about Hazel who appeared years younger but was easily recognizable in her gray dress. She was pleading with a small group of people who stood around a bonfire on a hot summery night. The sound of the river was loud, almost drowning out their voices. Then Hazel seemed to shout, "You can't just let him go. The river will swallow him, take him down." The people just laughed. Frances felt herself approach Hazel and reach for her arm. Hazel met her with a delighted grin. "Oh, I'm so glad you've come."

"I'm Frances."

"I know. I was certain you had heard my request. Even then I could see your glowing heart." And she pointed. Frances looked down as a radiant light poured from her chest, causing her to blink and shield her eyes with her forearm.

She sat up in bed to a room flooded by the overhead light, the dream over. "Sorry," whispered Ethel's voice, "I couldn't find my school book so I had to turn on the light. Oh there it is." The room went dark again.

"What time is it?"

"It's just after eleven. You've got hours of sleep in front of you so please don't hold a grudge. Everyone goes to sleep so early around here—except dad. Sorry to say he's at the sewing machine tonight."

Sure enough the hum of the small engine drove through the curtain and found Frances. She pressed one ear into her pillow and carefully, hoping not to disturb Carol, drew the quilt up over her other ear. The dream came back to her then and she tried to burrow her way back into it. When she awoke the next morning, Wednesday, it was still there.

∗

She dressed, ate a small breakfast and left the house. She noted, without giving it an actual glance, the continued existence of the elm tree, as she set out down the street. At the corner of Broadway and Emerson she looked into Feldman's

Jewelry Shop, saw that the windows were still dark, and so headed up the block. No one was at the phone booth so she hurried to it, dropping in a coin, and dialed Mr. Silverman's line. His voice brought a stab of indecision to Frances but she fought through it, explaining that she would be unable to work today. There hung a stretch of silence between them as she scrambled for a good excuse, distraught at having forgotten to prepare one. He spoke first, telling her what a good idea it was to take a day or two off.

Relieved she hung up the phone and began walking back in the direction she had come, past fingerprint smudges on store windows drenched in the morning sun, past a swirl of yellowed leaves skittering across the sidewalk, past the street sign on the corner, its pole speckled with rust. By the time she reached the jewelry store she could see Mr. Feldman moving about behind the glass counter. The bell on the door shook as she went in.

"Good morning," Mr. Feldman called, coming around to greet her. She eyed the satin texture of the back panel of his vest and saw that the small belt had come undone. She could tell he was studying her face trying to determine her name.

"Good morning. I'm Frances Lang, Walter and Mary's daughter."

"Of course," he sang. "Looking for a hatpin or a broach for your autumn coat?" He moved toward a case along the wall.

"Rather," she said, "I'm here just to ask a question."

He stopped. "Oh, I see."

"Well, I know it's a little out of the ordinary, but," she fumbled. "Well I wonder if you might tell me... You see I was on the streetcar, last Friday evening when the accident happened. I saw it all and I ran after the girl and I was holding her pocketbook when the man came and I tried to give it to him but he wouldn't take it."

She stopped abruptly, a far distance from her question. In fact, she realized with alarm, she didn't know exactly what she came to ask. He waited for her to continue. He pushed his glasses further up the bridge of his nose and cleared his throat twice.

"I didn't do it to snoop. I looked in her pocketbook for an address so I could return it and I found the name of your store written on a piece of paper. It struck me as odd because I didn't expect, well anyway..."

Mr. Feldman had used up a full morning of patience standing before the young lady. He had a watch to repair and an order to place. Any moment a customer could come in and he didn't want to be caught conversing about the colored girl's death. Unfortunate as it was, he didn't want any association with her or her fiancé who had lingered in his store far too long. What, he had wondered all week, had brought the boy into his store? He wasn't personally against selling a wedding ring to a colored man, he was just apprehensive of having colored clientele. He had worked hard, being Jewish on a street that didn't have many Jewish businesses, to establish himself as a fair and trustworthy jeweler and was determined to guard against any factor that might threaten his reputation.

"No Frances, she never came into my store," he said, as if there was nothing more to it. He hoped she would be discouraged and leave. She stood waiting for him to continue.

Feeling impatient and suddenly rather impulsive, he decided to tell her the rest. "The fellow who knew her, her fiancé, was in my store when the accident happened. He was waiting for her. He wanted to buy a wedding ring, but was waiting for her to come and pick it out." He paused, then added, "But she never did, never made it into my store."

He had meant for the last sentence to draw a conclusion to their discussion but once out of his mouth the words landed with a thud on the hard floor. In the midst of the quiet room he sensed, in a way he hadn't before, the gravity of the young woman's death and within the silent moment came to realize that a man's life had shattered into pieces.

She finally asked, "Did he tell you his name?"

"No, no, we didn't get that far."

"Her name," she said, finding it imperative that it should be known, "was Hazel." She buttoned up her coat and left the store, resisting the impulse to yell Hazel's name out to the people moving up and down the street. After she was gone, Mr. Feldman returned to his worktable. He sat for a good while before picking up his tiny tools and opening the broken watch.

*

Mrs. Schneider punched the dough with her fist, turned it on the floured table and began to knead it with her palm. She had placed her wedding ring in the shot glass on the window ledge. She only removed the band, with the three small diamonds embedded deep into the gold, on bread day. Sometimes she would forget to put it back on until late that night, amazed that she had proceeded through the day without noticing. The skin under the band was always a shade whiter and more delicate compared to the rest of her weathered hand. It brought to mind the long ago days when she had expected other things from life.

When the dough turned sticky, she added flour. She sprinkled a bit on the table as well. The two loaves she made every Wednesday lasted her and her husband a whole week. She often sang while she worked; soft and melodic until the chorus, when she liked to deliver the lines with zeal. She had decent pitch but her range was limited. This bothered her very little since she had learned from her first marriage that singing was for the singer, not for the ears who heard it. She could not imagine moving through her day without it or a Wednesday without baking bread. Her grandmother had taught her how to measure and sift and work the dough. They sang together, in German, about a hat with three corners.

Her first husband had squinted over the ridge of his eyeglasses and frowned when she sang. She considered waiting until he left the house but then opted for ignoring the frown. When he died in the first big war she decided it was his fault that they had been married for five years with no babies. She met Henry a decade later. He assured her it was not too late for children, but in time, she assured him it was.

"You have me, and I you. That is enough. Is it not, my sweet?" he had said in the most upbeat tone. Then he asked her to sing his favorite song.

As she placed two smooth mounds of dough in a bowl, covered it with a clean cloth to set upon the radiator to rise, she smiled. *My Henry*, she thought. Then she began his song, "What a difference a day makes. Twenty-four little hours..." But she did not get through the entire song before her mind landed on the Lang girl whom she had watched from the window the night before. She knew Frances had seen the entire streetcar accident. She shuddered to imagine such a death. Then she thought of the victim's mother. How could a mother endure such a thing? It must be worse to lose a child in such a way than not to have one at all. She looked up from the table.

"But I can't be sure of that," she murmured out loud. She forced her attention back to the bread and before she realized it, was singing her grandmother's song. "Mein Hut, der hat drei Ecken. Drei Ecken hat mein Hut," *Had it not three corners it would not be my hat.*

Frances plopped onto a park bench just a short way down the path that led into North Commons Park. She was roughly a half-mile from home and relieved to find a spot to rest. As comfortable as the flat brown shoes had seemed at the start of her journey, her arches now complained and there was an ache along her shinbone. She looked out upon the near empty park and thought about lunch. The cup of ginger tea she had shared with Camille Banks an hour earlier, was all she'd had since breakfast. But she would just have to suffer through a hunger pain or two and a dose of guilt from deceiving her mother. Here she was on a park bench while her mother believed her to be behind a desk downtown.

When the sunshine had traveled the full length of the bench and then dropped off, she began to feel stiff and restless. She wondered how else to spend the remainder of the afternoon. She wished she had packed a book. This thought brought to mind the public library. Of course, the perfect place to spend an afternoon—and with softer seats. She got up and then on impulse rummaged through her purse, finding a candy bar at the bottom. Her stomach rumbled as she opened the Walnut Hill and began to walk.

Within ten minutes she was up the steps of the North Regional Branch Library and into the damp-smelling building, slipping past Mrs. Decker who was curved over a stack of books that needed shelving. Frances found a quiet spot in Fiction between F and H on a lone stool adrift in the aisle. She pulled down a novel, by William Faulkner, that she had read once before. In fact, there weren't many books in the fiction section that she hadn't read or determined weren't worth reading. She had come to rely on the librarian to alert her to the arrival of any new novels, but in the meantime she had to settle for a second or third time with a favorite.

The cushioned chairs positioned in the open area of the library tempted her, but she opted for the solitude of the stool. Mrs. Decker would be sure to inquire as to why she was idling away a weekday afternoon. She opened the hard cover book to chapter eleven, being partial to the ending, and began. A few pages later, she could feel a fog begin to descend just below the line she was reading, making her progress painfully slow. Her chin too, wanted to give in to a downward pull. I'll just close my eyes for a moment she decided, easing against the metal bookshelf behind her.

Hours before, she had left the Banks' home not wanting to look back at the solemn face of Mrs. Banks watching her go. Yet she forced herself to turn and smile, surprised to find that the woman appeared tall from the edge of the front porch. Taller and somewhat brighter across the eyes. Perhaps it was the visit from Frances that persuaded the older woman to linger in the fresh air for a few moments. Frances wanted to think so; that the few words she offered about her daughter's last moments had proved helpful, in some small way. Moreover, she enjoyed the sense of having fulfilled an obligation that she could now set behind her. She had revealed Hazel's request; handed the words over to her mother, to have and to keep, as if they could fit inside a locket, snapped closed and given away. That Hazel's mother had not recognized the name Hollis, was a fact she felt certain she could dismiss with minor effort. Who knew how complicated relationships could be among some people? She couldn't pretend to guess how colored people really lived.

She now dozed, her neck carrying the weight of her bowed head, then awoke with a start due to the crashing sound of Mrs. Decker inadvertently toppling the book cart at the back of the library. She blinked a few times until she remembered where she was. Her eyes traveled over the dusty books stacked all around her, the faded colors of their spines holding each other up. She inhaled deeply, leaning back against the bookshelf again. She liked this place, the smell of old, musty paper mixed with the lingering scent of floor wax. She liked how quiet it was, especially now when there was no hum from the overhead lights that had yet to be turned on. She looked about imagining she could, by just sitting here, absorb the words of the pages around her and know their contents. She felt strangely open, her mind lucid, a sense of clarity moving through her in the muted, afternoon light. Within this clear space, came a realization. It sifted like snow until it shown cold and clear and could not be denied. She had not fulfilled her duty to Hazel Banks. Her earlier notion that she had was nothing but foolish. She had not found Hollis and she could not leave it up to someone else to do so. She had to keep trying. She was surprised that this thought did not frighten her.

She closed her eyes for another moment and imagined Hazel alive, walking along an avenue with a smile on her face and her hand reaching up to wave to a friend. *We* could have been friends, Frances thought. Yes, we could have been friends. This idea struck her so keenly that she got up from the stool and placed the book back on the shelf, knowing it was time to go.

✷

At four-thirty she slipped out of the library, down the block and turned onto Broadway. Passing the shoe store she glanced in to find Mr. Pearson looking out. He raised his hand in a sort of wave. She smiled and then noticed that Irene, Mr. Pearson's daughter, was also in the store. She decided to stop. She knew Irene too well to pass by without a hello. She also wanted to inquire about a lay-away plan for a new pair of shoes.

"Evening Frances," said Irene, the moment the door had opened. Mr. Pearson stood behind the register, off to the side.

"Evening."

"I was hoping you'd stop in," began Irene. "I haven't seen you in a coon's age and I really wanted to know how you were doing, especially after what happened last week. My father told me you saw the whole incident. I can hardly believe it. Are you still shaken-up over it? Poor thing."

The flood of attention felt good to Frances. Irene was only a few years older but had always assumed a doting role with her. When Frances began kindergarten, Irene had waited on the corner for her so they could cross the busy street together and continue on to school. There had even been a shoebox half-full of hair ribbons that Irene had passed on to her when she was still young enough to wear them.

She cleared her throat, "You might say I *am* still a bit shook-up. In fact, that seems the perfect description for how

I feel inside. Almost like a soda pop with the cap still on."

This thought forced a short, jerky laugh from Frances that sounded more like a hiccup. She quickly covered her mouth with the back of her hand, looking at her friend to see if the laugh registered as inappropriate as it felt. Irene did not smile but her expression was one of concern not disapproval.

Then she remembered the feeling of clarity she had found in the library and continued in a candid manner, "It's not every day someone dies in front of you."

Irene smiled. A sad, heartbroken smile. She wanted to reach out and hug Frances but didn't for fear it would bring on the tears that balanced on the edge of this, as well as every other, exchange of emotion. Irene had never been prone to crying until her young husband had left for the war.

Mr. Pearson closed the register and came out to stand next to his daughter. He had heard every word of the conversation and was ready to move the focus on to something less disturbing, like restocking the shoelace display.

"Although," said Irene, hoping to swing the discussion upward, "it's not as if you knew her. Imagine if it was someone from the neighborhood, someone from school, even a friend? Now that really would have been just awful."

Frances smiled at Irene, then looked at Mr. Pearson hovering near his daughter. On his face was a strange expression that she studied for a long moment, hoping for but not finding some sign of the compassion she sensed when he had knelt down with her next to Hazel. A second face had hardened, like a coat of varnish, over the one he wore days before. She turned back to Irene.

"She *was* like a friend. What I mean is, I think of her as a friend. Why wouldn't we have been friends?" She felt the surge of decisiveness rush up against the roof of her mouth. "And I intend to make it better. I intend to help her."

"What are you saying Frances?" came Mr. Pearson's voice, louder than usual. The disturbing feelings from the night of the accident came back to him. He had told himself that it had not been the dead girl's fault. She had been the victim, after all. But he had also found himself wondering what reason she had for being on his street, spilling over into his Friday, invading his thoughts. He had needed to blame the girl for what she had no business plastering to the back of his eyelids. Eventually the disquieting image of her lying in the street, dress torn, had dissolved. In its place a vague sense of affliction remained.

"It's too late to do anything for her now," he continued, steadying his voice. "You helped her all you could. You did more than expected, more than anyone would have expected."

"I didn't do anything exceptional Mr. Pearson. Same thing any decent person would have done."

With that statement any remnants of a need to ask about shoes moved deep into a new room inside Frances; a room for trivial things once deemed important. She nodded at Irene and left the store. As the door closed behind her she realized, with a thud, that it was true, she hadn't really done anything exceptional for Hazel. Worse, she had been gently milking the notion that she had.

Irene and her father followed Frances with their eyes as she moved passed the front windows. Both felt stung, as if caught outside in a blizzard, by the demeanor of the young woman they had both known for years. One, older and more afraid, was unwilling to let the meaning of her words perforate the convenient shield of surprise they held up between them.

"My goodness," was all Irene said before she forced her attention toward Little Timmy upstairs, who was due his dinner. She handed her father the metal shoehorn in her hand and headed toward the back of the store, wondering if her mother had gotten the meal started. Halfway up the stairs she folded into a ball and wept, for what exactly she didn't understand.

Frances, on the other hand, was fully absorbing the impact

of her own words as she turned onto her block. When she reached the yard she looked directly at the elm tree.

"I'll find him," was all she said. Then the door opened so Carol and Howard could rush out onto the front porch, encircling their big sister with arms and noise.

7

Cotton would not have made it to the Monday morning funeral if Miss Emma had not seen to it. Had he skipped it, as was his desire, he would have grabbed the duffel bag and prepared to leave while the house was empty. He would have counted his money and determined it was enough. Placed a cap on his head and made it as far as the front hall before images of Walter Lang, holding Hazel's pocketbook, would have stopped him and brought on a pacing across the hard floor. Moreover, he really had nowhere to go. He couldn't imagine setting out for someplace else when he had folded up all his hope, like a paper airplane, and flew it to this place just eight months ago. How could he start over again? Below his conscious thoughts dwelled the likelihood that he would miss this life, even without Hazel in it.

But Miss Emma spared him from such decisions as she laid out his pressed clothes, set the razor on the sink, buffed his only pair of shoes and nudged him down the hall toward the bathroom. While he was shaving she kicked the duffel bag, parked like a dilapidated car in the center of the room, deep under the bed where she deemed it belonged. She ran her hands along her apron, and nodded at how cooperatively it had slid across the floor.

∗

Miss Emma lived in this house since she was a child. There had been other dwellings that she and her seven siblings had filled with noise, but this one her parents had kept. It was the oldest house in the neighborhood; when first built, it was surrounded by nothing but woods. The four-bedroom

house had happily fit them all, including Granny, who ran
the kitchen while Emma's parents worked a variety of jobs
to ensure enough food and clothes for a house of ten. But
in the end, not one of her siblings had stayed in the area,
spreading out around the country, and so when her parents
passed and Granny before them, the house fell into her hands
alone. While it had been twenty years since the last sister had
left, she worked hard every day to recapture the feel of the
past. She filled the house with people, kept the furniture in
a set position, cooked from her grandmother's pots. When
the oil-backed tablecloth got a hole in it she searched until
she found a pattern nearly identical to the old one, and then
cut and hemmed it to the same dimensions. Each morning as
she stepped into the kitchen to prepare breakfast, she stood
a moment in the beam of sunlight reaching through the east
window and thought of her grandmother.

"Granny," Little Emma used to say, "Tell me again how
you came here."

"Oh no, child you ain't like to trick me no more. Not
through all that mess when you done known it good already."
But Granny, after a few minutes of peeling fruit with her par-
ing knife, would start in sighing and moving her lips until the
story would be in the room like the smell of the pears filling
Emma's nose.

She did know the story by heart. Granny had come up to
Minnesota as a girl, the year before the Emancipation Proc-
lamation. She had come for a whole summer when the lakes
were deep and clear, the sky overhead a sharp blue. She stood
each morning on a dock holding a white beach towel, only
once dipping her hand in when she pretended to shoo a deer-
fly away from her mistress's discarded sun hat. The master sat
fat-bellied on a rocking chair pulled from the cabin out to the
lawn. She could hear his snoring from where she stood sweat-
ing on the dock.

When the vacation ended and the time came to return

to Missouri, she walked submissively toward the railroad station lugging the over-packed bags. She could not imagine the ride back down the tracks. The monotony of the cramped boxcar relegated to her and a half dozen other slaves, rocked against any remnants of caution she had left. Worse, the end of the journey promised accommodations just as bleak. Busy arguing over the price of their return tickets, the sun-kissed couple did not notice when the young girl slipped into the crowd and then into the back of a wagon waiting to cart her to a place that could hide her for the six remaining months of legalized slavery. She could not say what measures the couple took to get her back, nor did she care.

Little Emma watched her grandmother's gnarled hands chop the pears into small chunks that would cook down swiftly into sauce. As an adult, Miss Emma picked from a new crop of pear trees in the back yard, but while her pear sauce brought compliments from her boarders, it did not match in flavor that which she remembered from Granny's big wooden spoon. In fact, none of her attempts to recapture the gaiety and exuberance of her childhood seemed to fully work. She needed her tenants but secretly begrudged them for, what seemed to her, their strange and subdued habits. She kept herself busy, accomplishing the household tasks with efficiency and flare. The staircase banister gleamed with polish, the aroma from her meals drifted toward the windows of envious neighbors, and the citrus-scented sheets were stretched across their mattresses with perfect hospital corners. Regardless of her effort, she could not root out the sense of betrayal in being left alone. Once, when younger and optimistic, she had toyed with the thought of loving a man from St. Paul. But he had proven reckless with her feelings and she had to spit on his shoes to get him to leave. She preferred to be alone than to run the risk of disloyalty.

Then Cotton arrived. She had come to imagine him as her son. She would do what she could to keep him near. She recognized immediately that he was important, that he was an example of happiness. She loosened her clutch on the hard feelings that she had lined along the walls of her house in the shape of furniture. She over-cooked the asparagus and laughed when no one seemed to notice. She skipped Wednesday evening prayer group one week in order to watch the sun set from the front steps.

✳

Cotton returned from the bathroom, his body feeling thick and hard to command. He found clothes spread out on the bed and slowly began to dress. He was relieved to have someone directing him through the morning and although he moved a few beats behind Miss Emma's instructions he found himself, hours later, on the front porch of the Banks' home, the funeral service over. He lowered his head and crossed the threshold with Miss Emma at his elbow. She kept an eye on him, though he moved about very little. He smiled a borrowed smile at those who spoke to him. He stood for a time and then sat, holding a plate of untouched food in his right hand. When he overheard one of the neighbors recall how much Hazel had liked to skip rope in her Sunday dress, he fixed his gaze to the leg of the coffee table and bore his attention into it. Miss Emma, after a while, took the plate out of his hand.

Camille, and Lewis too, kept him in view while they drifted through the rooms of the house, murmuring to little groups of people dressed in black. They were both worried about him, their almost son, but had nothing at this point to offer him.

Around quarter past four, the thought of Hazel's bedroom popped into his head. He squeezed it back out, but it returned. He had never been in it, only passed by on the Saturday afternoon he had built the bookshelves, barely stealing a glimpse as Mr. Banks was merely a creaking floorboard away and working a hammer. The urge to see it clung now to his lungs. He coughed but it didn't help. Miss Emma, clearing an empty platter from the table, disappeared into the kitchen, the door swinging behind her. He was to the stairs before he decided to move. By the time he reached the top step and turned toward her room, Miss Emma hadn't even found a serving spoon for the macaroni. Camille, on the other hand, was listening for his footsteps above her head. She did not send her husband to follow him. Lewis, although caught in conversation, heard not only the footsteps but also the door creak and then silence.

Cotton kept his hand on the knob, as he peered into the room. Hazel's bed was near the window with a table next to it holding an empty glass and a stack of books piled under a small lamp. A dress was strewn across a chair in the corner. Her closet door was ajar. He inhaled. He could smell the powder that she wore. He could detect, in fact, a light dusting of it on the floor around the chair that held the crumpled dress.

He found his legs would not lead him further into the room, so he lowered himself down onto the small throw rug on which he had been standing. Kneeling, he then brought his forehead to the floor and stayed in that position for such a long minute that when he heard voices near the bottom of the stairs behind him, he wondered if he had, for just a moment, been asleep. Or not asleep, but missing, gone somewhere from this spot. The strange sensation passed so quickly that it seemed to dismiss itself from his mind before he could decide what to do with it. It was not important, yet suggested another thing beyond his grasp.

He rose slowly, looking through the window near her bed to see the boarding house, his window winking back at hers. His hand on the knob again he looked once more at the chair, then under it, where the powder seemed like a layer of dust. Even the scent, now, was less convincing.

He shut the door. Had he gone in and lowered his head onto Hazel's pillow he might have found a place where he belonged, where he experienced a moment of symmetry in contrast to the disjointed world that spun him into one wrong moment after another. Or he may have discovered his feelings of discord remained despite her soft pillow. This he could not risk. He was not strong enough, yet, to attempt to feel better and fail.

He headed for the staircase without but a glance into the one room whose door stood wide open, the room that just days ago promised to be a library. His eye took a snapshot of the books scattered amidst the boxes, the bare bookshelf and the silence that held it together. Then the shutter of his eye closed and he descended to the crowded lower floor of the house.

*

The morning after the funeral Miss Emma insisted that he get to work on time. She made a point of arguing the importance of punctuality so as to obscure the real issue of Cotton choosing not to go at all. She woke him early. She handed him his clothes, set his boots by the bed.

"I sent Ralph down yesterday to let him know," she said. "Boss says he expects you today. I packed your lunch now and breakfast is waiting downstairs. Set my day off wrong to see a breakfast go cold, you head on down." She glanced out the window and added, "Feels to me like some clouds might roll in today. Can't tell by looking though, blue everywhere."

He made it to the table but stalled halfway through a piece of buttered toast, as if the fourth corner was too heavy to lift from his plate. He dropped the toast to the plate and turned his gaze out the back door.

"You can't sit around here son. It ain't good for you. Get up in that job and work some, it'll help move the heaviness through and you'll be better for it. That part you can't hang on to, sugar. That the part that'll drag you down."

So he went to work on Tuesday, and the next day as well. He moved in the direction she pointed and found some comfort in routine. At work he didn't speak to anyone, he spent lunch breaks near the river, fighting off the urge to draw Hazel's face on the paper sack that held his uneaten sandwich. He worried he might lose it forever, but it felt discrepant to chance something beautiful emerging from such pain.

He had been drawing secretly since he was young. He had read next to nothing on technique; composition, contrast, style. He could not name an artist that he felt his work resembled, not having read a single book on art history or modern art. In fact he had not shown a soul his work, yet he nonetheless felt rather certain it was good. He held to this opinion not because the act of drawing afforded him such a deep sense of satisfaction but because, after hiding them away for months, even years, the revisited drawings leapt off the paper, knocking his insides out. They assured him the world was beautiful. One day he would add color to his work and be flooded with a sense of pleasure that would make the need to share it outweigh the fear that had kept him from doing so thus far.

On this Wednesday, far before he touched a paintbrush to canvas, he sat along the riverbank and let memories of Hazel float across the front of his thoughts. As each new image came, he mourned the one drifting away. Slow like butter, his mind churned until it struck the wall of sorrow, too ancient and familiar not to bring forth the ache he harbored for his mother. He struggled under the weight of losing them both. This unjustness, more than anything else, had shackled itself to his limbs over the past few days. He was full of self-pity and made no attempt to rebuke himself for it.

"Why?" he asked aloud to the moving water. "Why would life be so unfair?" He wanted an apology. He wanted the earth to buckle under him, the sky to crack open, the sun to shrink. He wanted train whistles silenced, streetcars derailed, store windows smashed. He wanted the driver of the pickup truck found. He had considered demanding they search for the man responsible for Hazel's death, but as yet, could not trust

himself in front of an averse police department. He thought
of Feldman's Jewelry Store and ground his teeth. Why had
he suggested they meet there? Why Friday? Why not go on
Saturday, together? If only he had picked the ring out himself
and surprised her with it.

He threw a stick into the river.

And his mother, why did she go so soon? Dying from in-
fluenza when he was only two, before she had the chance to
raise him or give him a sibling. Before she had the chance
to see him run with speed, jump over a fence or sketch his
first butterfly. Before he could do much but totter around
behind her. He envisioned himself following her, reaching up
for her apron. She had taught him that much, he suddenly realized. She must have seen him crawl and then learn to walk,
to babble and to hit a spoon against a pot to make noise. She
had enough time to love me, he thought. To hold me, nurse
me, laugh when I squealed. She was there in the beginning, in
the making of me. He was so struck by this discovery that his
body began to shake. He sobbed into his hands, crying in a
way that released a disappointment that had pressed under his
breastbone for years. "She knew me," he said out loud, "even
if I don't remember her, *she knew me.*"

He stood and stretched his limbs, his arms reaching out.

And she had known him, if only for a quick wink of time,
before he and his father ended up alone in a one-room house,
front door opening to nothing but fields and sky. Days that
began before sun-up and row upon row of white, beautiful,
despicable cotton to be picked and planted and picked again,
never on soil that he nor his father would own. He was strong
and agile, qualities a youth might use for play but for which
he gave away to the field for nothing in return but the nick-
name Cotton—because by fourteen he could harvest more
bags by day's end than most grown men. There had been a
hole in the floorboard in the middle of their room, a hole that
dropped into darkness and released the smell of wet earth.

There had been a window that rattled when the train rushed by, just feet from the back of the house. Years of a noise that never ceased to alarm him.

When he finished school, there seemed to be nothing left. He was supposed to feel lucky he had made it through the eighth grade, an education usually reserved for children of preachers or landowners, not families who needed every able body all year long. But he didn't feel lucky; grateful that his father let him finish, yes, but not lucky.

Months of hard work dragged into years and soon he was a grown man with a sinking feeling that there might be nothing more than the little he had, unless he took precautions. In the mornings, he crossed the dirt road into the field that owned his body. But at night, with an appetite for learning and a propensity for drawing, he returned to his books and his pencils. People called him strange. The women in the town embarked regularly on the topic of why such a graceful man, with an exceptional smile, refused to do anything but work. He was only spotted at the dry goods store, occasionally in church and never at the pool hall, not even to use the town's only telephone, mounted on the back wall. They wondered if he had ever traveled the eleven miles, crossing the bridge over the Mississippi River, and stepped foot in Memphis. Wasn't he the slightest bit curious about Beale Street?

In fact, Cotton's curiosity was boundless, which is why he plowed through the stacks of books lent to him by the Reverend's wife, thrilled to find a text with illustrations he could copy. Furthermore he *had* made it to Beale Street, where the music meant so much it hurt. A young man named Rufus Thomas had stood on a makeshift stage and sang straight to the back of Cotton's soul. He had left stunned, in the street endured the insults of two boys his same age but different color, and vowed not to return. It was easier to stay composed in a place like Sunset with only one main street and no post office, especially if he narrowed his world to work and home. He worried about giving pieces of himself away and in return letting the town seep into the open spaces that used to be him. There was the thought of one particular girl, however, who lived over on Sutter's Plantation, which kept at him. But he had promised himself the chance at somewhere else, so he fought it.

One night after the sun had sunk out of sight and the frogs had begun to sing, Cotton's father asked his son where the Mississippi River started.

"Minnesota," Cotton replied, setting his book down in his lap. He had been reading to his father from *Huckleberry Finn*. "Why?"

His father took a moment to gather up a string of neglected words, "I sure ain't fixin' to let you take it downward so best start thinking on following it up."

He stared at his father who nodded, then added, "I'm sorry boy; I done kept you too long."

Later that evening as Cotton rinsed the sweat and grime of the day's work from his face and then changed his shirt, Lewis Banks stood near the kitchen table in his own home gripping the back of a chair as his knuckles paled. "I can't give away another shift, so looks as if I'll leave early Friday morning. Be back on Tuesday." His wife stood at the stove stirring something that had not yet released its aroma. He continued despite her lack of response. "Have you considered asking my sister Ivy to come up for a while and stay? You know she'd come, if asked, and it may turn out to be right helpful, seeing as how I'll come and go so much."

"Perhaps," she whispered, not turning around.

"Tomorrow morning I'm planning to stop down at the police station and get in a word, this time with the Captain," he said.

"Oh, Lewis," she responded in the same hushed voice.

"I'm determined to try. How could I not pursue it Camille?"

"Because it won't get you anywhere. You filled out the report like they asked. They don't care what really happened. It's over for them." She was right and he would come to accept this, but only in time.

"Not if I insist they stay with it. Not if I insist they keep the case open. It's only just. If it was anyone else, any of their daughters, they would."

Now she turned to face her husband.

"It won't bring her back," she said and then decided by the look on his face, the pain radiating from the back of his eyes, not to tell him what she had learned earlier that day during the visit from the young woman who she reluctantly invited inside for a cup of tea. She had learned that their daughter had been dragged to her death behind the vehicle. To envision Hazel being hit by a pickup truck was bad enough, dragged behind it was too much for the imagination to hold. She wanted to spare Lewis from that. Then she wondered, suddenly, why the police had not informed him of such a fact. Maybe they had, she thought, and he had kept it from her.

"Do what you need to Lewis, just be careful."

It was quiet for a spell, a long moment that reminded them both of how empty the house was without their daughter.

"We had a visitor today," she began. "The daughter of the man who dropped off the pocketbook on Sunday."

He raised an eyebrow, waiting for her to continue.

"Well?" he said, finally. Then remembered that he had yet to ask her why their daughter had stashed forty dollars in the lipstick tube he found in her purse. He had unrolled the bills and placed them in his breast pocket, comforted by their presence, before later giving the purse over to Camille. He reminded himself to fetch them from the soiled shirt before washday.

"Turns out Hazel spoke to this girl, right after the accident. She asked this girl for, well, I guess you might say a favor."

"What kind of favor?" he said, patiently holding to the back of the chair, despite a small surge of adrenaline that ran through his fingertips. It had been impossible to cultivate a sense of urgency, let alone interest, in anything since his daughter's death. But as he stood waiting for his wife he was aware of a growing desire to want to know what she would say next. It caused him to step forward and touch his wife's arm.

"Please, go on."

She hesitated. She had anticipated disclosing to him all the information Frances had delivered, but suddenly felt the impulse to keep some of it for herself. It was like a star gone astray, streaking away from her. A remnant of her daughter that might last a moment longer if she didn't have to share it. She had for days been expecting, as she entered a room or reached the landing at the top of the stairs, to catch a glimpse of something in which Hazel remained. The sheer curtains, the mirror in the hall, the gleam off a serving plate. Now, the two words that she received earlier that afternoon felt akin to what she had been looking for. Who Hollis was paled next to the idea that Hazel had left behind something small but nearly solid for her mother to hold.

She would tell him tonight, she reasoned. A few more hours and the words that felt like pearls in her hand would be dull as stones, easier to give away. Even in this moment, as she looked at Lewis who was still waiting for her to speak, it was fading. She felt too tired to remember what was important and what was not.

She sighed just as the doorbell rang. It was Cotton. The memory of a wedge of pecan pie on a small plate had drawn him over.

8

The door to the jewelry story closed with a thud behind her, the sound of the tiny bell left for only Mr. Feldman to hear. Once on the street, in the morning air, she contemplated what to do next. She could catch a streetcar downtown and then get on the Glenwood line, but that would mean traveling right through Film Row. She couldn't risk passing Verle on her cigarette break or one of the brokers heading for a meeting. The walk, she reasoned, would do her good. Thankful for her comfortable old brown flats, she set off. She reached Sixth Avenue, just as she began to grow weary. From here she knew it was two more blocks until Fourth. She wished, suddenly, that she had another mile to go, uncertain of what this morning had driven her out of bed to accomplish.

She slowed, seeing that the few pedestrians around her were no longer white. How odd, she thought, to have lived twenty years and seldom encountered people with dark skin. And had not, until Hazel boarded the streetcar and now in this moment, really been aware of this fact. Granted there was an occasional man walking downtown or even in front of her office building, and she remembered a few times her father opening the back door to find a weary, weatherworn brown face asking for a sandwich. They must have come up from the river, like so many of the other men who camped at its edge, waiting for their luck to change, after word tumbled down the banks that the back door of the corner house on Bryant Avenue provided at best a sandwich, at least a warm greeting and a day-old biscuit.

She continued up Fourth Avenue toward the house number she'd memorized, her father having traveled this same path, three days before.

✳

Sunday morning he had set out just as Mary and the children left for mass. Enjoying the crisp morning walk, his gait was efficient but unhurried. Actually, he found the journey so pleasant he needed to remind himself more than once of his somber destination and to save his whistling for a different day.

Over the course of his lifetime, Walter had walked every street that ran through the north side of Minneapolis, not giving much thought to the south side, with its string of lakes and elaborate houses. He felt at home over north and he considered, not exclusively but possessively, all of it to be his own. He had come through this small neighborhood several times on his way to somewhere else. In fact, he knew of the path through the woods that led to the train tracks, having followed them on occasion to reach the outskirts of the city where he could view the wide expanse of farm fields. He had even worked not far from here during the Depression as part of the Public Works Administration. He had been hired to help clear out businesses and homes for the Sumner Field Project, the first public housing project in Minnesota, although it never had felt right to tear down people's lives even with the intention of putting up a housing development.

As he continued he passed a small grocery store and a barbershop, touching his cap to any man who would look him in the eye. Soon he was on the Banks' block. As he neared the house, he unzipped the front of his jacket and reached in for the pocketbook, glad that the cooler weather had required a jacket and relieved him from having to travel through town with a lady's purse in hand. Furthermore, it felt more respectful to keep Hazel's belongings discretely out of sight. He climbed the front steps, unaware that Cotton watched him from an upstairs window three houses away. He rang the doorbell. The sound triggered a twist of nervousness in his belly. He waited, not feeling it proper to ring again. Finally the door creaked open and Lewis Banks's face appeared, behind him the house was dark.

"Hello there, my name is Walt Lang. I'm sorry, sorry to bother you and even, of course, more so for your loss." He looked down at his shoes and then back up at Lewis. He imagined, with alarm, losing one of his children. He felt a surge of shame for having so thoroughly enjoyed his walk. "It's just that I came over because, see, my Frances she was on the streetcar and she seen what happened. She knelt down with your daughter but there wasn't, I'm afraid, too much she could do. Frances seemed to say your daughter didn't take but a few breaths. Well, I guess I'm telling you all this so you might know she didn't suffer long."

Lewis's face didn't change. It looked to Walter as if the man wasn't convinced that any of this information warranted being bothered by a stranger.

He remembered, then, the pocketbook and held it up. "And this, this belonged to your daughter."

He assumed that Lewis didn't normally pay much attention to the accessories Hazel collected, but even so, he watched how the sight of the small gray bag crushed the last remaining light in the man's eyes. Lewis finally nodded, opened his mouth as if to say something and then closed it again, reaching for the pocketbook.

Walter nodded in return and descended from the porch. Once on the public sidewalk he turned back, sensing he was still being watched, but the door was closed. He moved along the block feeling as if all superfluous emotions had been gutted out of him, what few remained pressed against his ribs. He ached, suddenly, for the scent of his children as babies. For their small, chubby bodies, their gurgling laughter, their obliviousness to the inevitable chaos to come. How is a father to protect them?

He was startled out of his thoughts by a shout and then noticed a young man in a white shirt bounding toward him.

"I know you, mister," the man hollered, despite being only a few strides away.

Walter widened his stance.

"I know you," Cotton repeated. He clenched his fingers and then released, clenched and released. "You remember? We met on the bridge and you seen fit to advise me on the best fishing spot along the river."

Walter remembered, having been impressed by the young man's manners and intrigued by the way the ends of his words slid off into nothingness. Early one evening, nearly a month ago, they had struck up a conversation on the Broadway Bridge. He recalled how the boy leaned his elbows on the wide, stone ledge overlooking the moving water, as if there was no better place to be.

"And then you told me about a jewelry store up along Broadway, saying I'd find something real nice for my girl."

Walter remained silent waiting for a clue from Cotton and hoping for clarity from his own recollection to help explain why the man seemed a different person. A seed of indignation was blooming in Walter's belly, too small for him to name. Had it grown any bigger, he would have recognized, with some dismay, that he did not appreciate being spoken to in such a tone by a colored man. It would have surprised him to know he harbored, tiny but anchored, remnants of the same attitude he found disagreeable in others.

Sensing a stirring within and realizing that Cotton's voice had reached an impasse somewhere deep in his throat, he grabbed the chance to ask, "Of course, did something go wrong? Did Mr. Feldman not…"

Instantly, he realized his oversight. He had assumed Cotton would be treated fairly and graciously and had not given a thought to the likelihood that Mr. Feldman might let prejudice taint their exchange. Had Mr. Feldman, Jewish after all, turned the young man out?

"Oh, I see now," he began, without much air in his lungs. "I can see why you'd be sore about it. I really didn't think..."

"No," growled Cotton. "No you don't see, you don't see why I'm sore. I ain't sore, mister. That's the funny thing. There's nothing left here that can bruise. It's all steel now, right through from front to back." And he thumped a fist against his chest. But even as he said it the skin on his face slid further into sadness, his eyes slouched.

He continued, "Know what I was after? What I'd been waiting on all these years? One morning with her and not another soul in the world calling my name, no place else I needed to go. A pool of sunshine round my bed and her. Now that's gone, any chance of it. Now every morning will be just like this one, full a nothing, empty."

Walter, puzzled, lifted his hands. Then his confusion parted so that at once he envisioned Hazel—the woman he imagined her to be—sitting with Cotton on the edge of a bed. Walter's arms sunk down to his sides as the realization flooded over him. It would take the solitude of his walk home to attempt to piece together the remaining facts but he knew now why Cotton stood before him looking so battered. Were there words he could offer the young man? Before he could grab a hold of even one, Miss Emma arrived.

A minute of her urging convinced Cotton to return to the house, his anger dissolving into another bout of grief. After she had spotted him from the parlor window, saw his wrinkled shirttail and elbows held too wide in front of the white man, she bound down the sidewalk toward them. She had been listening all morning for signs of movement from his room upstairs. She had even forgone Sunday church, in case he needed her. But when she had stepped out to the backyard to scatter a stale piece of bread for the birds, she had missed his noisy descent down the stairs and out the front door.

Walter nodded to the woman, but did not touch his cap.

He witnessed her smooth Cotton's shirtsleeve with the pads of her fingers and say "come on" as if she was gently easing a toddler toward his nap. Only when she had Cotton turned around did she look back at Walter and return a penny worth of a nod.

✳

Frances, three days later, still knew nothing of the Sunday encounter except that the pocketbook had been returned. She had no idea that her father and Hazel's fiancé had crossed paths, twice. Nor that Cotton's curiosity over Walter's connection to the accident would, in part, keep Cotton from hopping a train out of town. Thus, she had no inclination to look up at Miss Emma's second story window on Wednesday morning as she crept along Fourth Avenue. She arrived in front of the Banks' home at such an increasingly slow pace that she didn't realize she had been standing a full minute, staring at three licorice-colored numbers tacked to the house, before the door opened.

Camille had been expecting Frances, ever since Sunday when her husband had shown her the pocketbook and described the conversation with the man who had delivered it. She knew the white man's daughter would come around, too laden with guilt not to return the money. First thing she had found, after Lewis had left the room, was the lipstick case empty of the bills she had helped Hazel roll. What did she care, if the money was gone? But she did. Hadn't they taken enough? she had cried into the satin lining of the bag.

It didn't make sense that a person who lacked the moral fiber to resist stealing two twenty-dollar bills from a dead woman's purse would then decide to confess, but she needed to believe that the girl would come. She needed to believe that one day soon there would be a knock on the door with some sort of explanation behind it to lessen the anguish that clawed at her skin and tugged at the roots of her hair since her daughter's death. The small funeral service and the burial at the wind-swept cemetery had done nothing to help her and while the grief-stricken days rolled one into another, she found herself waiting—perhaps for the sheer distraction that it allowed.

"Morning," Frances offered.

"Hmmph."

"My name is Frances Lang. That was my father who came by a few days ago to offer his condolences and then, also to return the pocketbook."

"I know who you are," came the response. "I know why you've come." Her stomach churned.

"Oh." Frances swallowed. "Gosh, I don't see how you could know why, since I didn't mention a thing to my father about it."

"Seems like you wouldn't." Camille wasn't exactly enjoying being rude. Still it felt necessary.

"Well no, I didn't tell anyone. I guess I've been trying to figure things out for myself. Trying to understand what Hazel's words meant."

At the mention of her daughter's name, her ears filled with the sound of the ocean. She thought to shake her head.

"What I mean is," Frances raced on, "when the man got there and picked her up, I thought that must be all she was asking for but then a few days later I... Well I had a dream and I just couldn't leave it alone without checking."

"What are you saying, miss?"

"I'm not being clear at all, am I?" Frances's distress gripped at the muscles in her lower back. She closed her eyes against the echo of her disconcerted explanation. "What I'm trying to tell you is, I ran up to her just after the accident. See, I was on the streetcar. I started to get off at the same stop and, trying to be polite, I waited for her to go first. If I hadn't, well if I hadn't everything would be... would be different. Seems like my skirt was cut more narrow so it might not have caught on the truck and in any case it would have all happened differently."

She had vowed that she wouldn't relay this part of the story, that she would just stick to Hazel's request. But now she was crying in front of a woman whose angry tone had provoked much more.

"Come inside."

She sat in silence while Camille filled the teapot, peeled the skin off a gingerroot, chopped it, and tossed it at the bottom of two teacups before pouring in the boiling water.

"It'll help your stomach," said Camille, hers still upset. She sat down across from Frances who now looked so young and fragile.

Finally, she spoke, "The fact is my daughter was hit by a vehicle that you were not driving. All that other business about who was supposed to step off the streetcar first, is nonsense. Now let's get to the point. What's this about my daughter speaking to you?"

The air whistled lightly through Frances's nose. "Like I was saying, I ran up to her right after her dress tore away from the pickup truck."

"Her dress was caught on the truck?"

"In the back fender. When she stepped into the street, the truck seemed to just sweep her away. But the dress tore within a few moments and the truck continued on as if it didn't know anything had happened."

"So she wasn't actually hit by the truck?"

"No." Frances had to force the next line out. "She was dragged behind it."

Mrs. Banks's expression divided into fragments but she did not retract her gaze. Frances felt she should continue. She told her about the people who gathered in a ring around them and Mr. Pearson, too shaken to be of any help.

"By then Hazel wasn't breathing. It wasn't more than half a minute from when I got to her, she slipped away."

Camille pressed a hand over her mouth, yet nodded for Frances to proceed.

"But before the crowd, before Mr. Pearson, I knelt down beside your daughter. She opened her eyes and that's when she spoke. She said, "Find Hollis." Well, I don't have to tell you how that perplexed me and I felt all together inept, not knowing what to do."

"That's all she said?"

"Yes. She fixed her eyes on me real hard for a while and then they closed."

Camille stood up, lifted her teacup and poured the tepid liquid down the sink, then placed the cup on a shelf inside the cupboard. She peered out through the one kitchen window and waited for a black bird, perched on the clothesline pole, to caw.

"I was relieved when Hollis came," Frances said, "knowing how Hazel had asked for him. Even though it was too late, I'm sorry it was too late, yet still it somehow seemed better." She, too, gazed out the window but from her seated angle saw only sky.

Camille turned back around, realizing, as she stared at the bobby pin in the young woman's hair, that she found her incapable of having taken the money.

"I guess you're wondering why I've come, then?" Frances asked, stretching the corner of her coat across her knees.

"You said you had a dream?" Camille asked. "A dream that suggested you hadn't quite helped Hazel like you thought?"

"Yes, that's right."

"The reason why you feel that way is because the man you saw, the man she was about to marry, is named Cotton, not Hollis."

The room held silent. The bird outside flew off.

"Then who is Hollis?"

Camille's voice turned hoarse. "I can't say. That, for the life of me, I can't say."

II

9

The leaves turned their colors and then detached from the trees until there was nothing left but the dull brown branches against a long stretch of mostly overcast skies. October passed and half of November before the first snowfall arrived. It began one late afternoon, picking up force by evening. Howard and Carol stared out the window, their breath fogging the panes so that they needed to wipe away the mounting excitement with their shirtsleeves.

Not until she was out hiking in the sifting, silent world with her father and two youngest siblings, dinner settling in their bellies, did Frances begin to suspect the significance of the night. Dusk falling, a hush settled on the roofs of the houses, the chrome door handles of parked cars, the rails of porches and the tops of warped garbage cans. The streetlights emitted a flurried glow that led Walter Lang and his children down toward the river to watch the open water lick the snow into its churning mouth. The makeshift tents that dotted the riverbank in warmer weather were gone. Frances wondered where the men, poor and mostly colored, found shelter when the weather turned bitter. She would have liked to imagine them hopping a train west. The more observant, the more thoughtful she became, the more difficult to spin the simple conclusions about strangers' lives that she had previously been so apt to do.

She had been determined, after her realization amongst the bookshelves of the library, and her promise to the immobile trunk of the elm tree, that she would continue to search for Hollis. She had waited, for weeks, for something to happen that might give her a direction in which to search. She hoped for another dream but her dreams, when Hazel appeared in them, were vague and sketchy. Despite her intentions, her old life had eased in around her like a worn shawl that, after a while, she grew tired of shirking off. At work and at home her routine caught along a grooved path. She was not the same person and yet everything around her seemed determined to tell her otherwise. Until this night, when the beauty of the first snowfall reminded her to be diligent.

The family stood on the bridge overlooking the Mississippi river bundled in layers, knit stocking caps and double mittens. The distant sound of the churning water and the frenzy of the falling snowflakes unable to escape their doom captured the group's attention. But at one point, Frances looked down the length of the bridge toward the other end and saw a lone figure standing where she hadn't noticed anyone before. Had it been a dog silhouetted against the lavender sky, or an abandoned bicycle, she would have been equally entranced by the contrast of its motionless body and the magic that swirled around it. But it was more than just the aesthetic appeal of a figure outlined against a flurried sky. If they were to walk closer, she would discover the man himself, looking out over the water, part of the reason the allure of the night had succeeded in gaining her acute attention.

As of late, when Cotton's workday ended he did not feel inclined to return to the boarding house, to his room with its sagging bed and long window. Especially now, in November, when the sun dropped out of the sky in the four o'clock hour and no trace of a sunset remained by the time the workers were released from the warehouse. The early darkness seemed to remove any necessity to adhere to the hands of a clock and he found himself willing to follow whatever path his boots chose to take. Miss Emma would keep his dinner warm regardless of the time he arrived. Night is night, he thought, and let it pull him toward the stone bridge.

Behind him, the voices of the men heading to Stanley's for a beer swept across the snowy distance and tapped at him between the shoulder blades. As of yet, he had never been asked to go along and would not have agreed to an invitation had it been offered. Nonetheless, their laughter followed him until he turned a corner and was suddenly alone on a quiet side street. The snow had begun hours earlier, forcing his well-soled boots to claw for the sidewalk hidden below the growing layer of white powder. Snowflakes collected across the black wool of his coat.

As he walked he began to sense how the blanket of snow, the first of the season, distinguished this night from others. There was a peculiar mix of cold and soft, of movement and silence. The whiteness fell into the places that had earlier been hard and bare. He noticed on all sides of him that objects, identifiable by name, were skewed in shape and size by a layer of snow rising up like a top hat or meringue on a lemon pie. The objects held their place, as if determined to be noticed. As if their altered appearance might become permanent if he voted it so or, even better, captured it with his pencil and sketch book.

He said a prayer of thanks for the snow. Prayer did not come easily to him but such a night seemed to require gratitude. He lifted his face to the wet flakes that had, for the moment, disguised the world he struggled to get through.

He searched out moments like this, days or nights that seemed to cast a new perspective on old routines. When nature reminded him that life could feel different if he tilted his head to one side, if snow cushioned his step, if an afternoon rain could wash the world anew.

✷

Four years earlier, at age twenty-one, he had witnessed such a rainstorm. It was 1940 and President Roosevelt had recently established a peacetime draft, the first in U.S. history. Cotton had studied the newspaper for a week to gather all the information he could on the subject, finding no race-based restrictions. All men between the ages 18 to 30 were required to register. But it was not clear, given the nature of segregation, what role someone like him might play as an enlisted man in the military. After rolling the idea around in his head that this could be a ticket out of the south, he raised the subject with his father.

"Son, we pick cotton in the Arkansas Delta. That man ain't letting the government take you off his plantation."

He was right. If Cotton had gone to the courthouse to register, the first question out of the sheriff's mouth would have been who did he work for and then an admonishment for upstaging his employer's authority. It was not for black men in that region to assume such a decision about their own future was theirs, regardless of some act signed by a president.

Nevertheless he decided to travel two towns over where he was unknown to the sheriff to see for himself if there was any chance of putting his name down. After seven miles of walking, he found a small building with grimy windows and inside it a door down a hallway with a cardboard sign tacked to it reading *Selective Service Board*. He did not pause until he had stepped into the slender light of the room. A ceiling fan moved dead air in slow, hot circles. The blue green walls suggested a false coolness that did not exist. He saw before him a flimsy table with two men propped on the chairs behind it. In front of each was a sandwich and a Nehi cola. A stack of papers and one ballpoint pen had been pushed down to the end of the table.

"Boy?" one man asked, using his hand to wipe at his mouth. His fingers were unusually long and his knuckles pressed hard against their skin.

Cotton stood with his arms at his sides, an ocean of silence gathering between him and the two men. A vinegary voice broke through.

"You soft in the head or somethin'?" the second man said. He had thick red hair that was cropped short but would have waved around his face had he worn it long like he did as a young child. His mother had run her fingers through it and called him Samson when her husband wasn't around. But one day his father had snipped off each lock as if he were pruning bushes, sneering at his wife through bared teeth. The curls never returned, while the sneer was passed along.

"You been asked a question that you ain't took to answer."

"No, sir, I'm not soft in the head," Cotton said.

The man stood up and tucked his shirt into his pants. Missing a belt loop, the end of the leather belt swung out like a snake's head until he caught it and held it against his waist. Most days he used a rope to keep his pants up, but today something convinced him to go fancy. Around the limp collar of his shirt, his neck was red and bumpy from the heat.

Cotton waited. The man with the knuckles glanced at the pile of papers at the end of the table, then back at Cotton. But the red haired man started up again.

"I know you didn't come in here figuring to sign-up for something when you see I got a sandwich and a soda drink losing fizz cause I'm made to stand here explaining that we ain't collecting names to win a pie at the church raffle? This here is where we take down men fit to fight in wars."

Red kept his hand against the belt as he shifted his weight from foot to foot. He found the belt distracting but he tried not to let it ruin the moment. "Now seeing as I don't know you from 'round here I'm assuming you stumbled in by accident. Am I right or not on that boy, 'cause I sure hate to be wrong? If you in some kind a trouble with the law and aiming to get you a soldier's uniform to hide in, I'll run you out a town so fast your head'll spin. But say you just wandering 'round looking to sign up for Sunday's pie give-away, I got an answer for that too. We don't put nigger names on the list even if we had a pie we was fixin' to raffle off."

Cotton felt an urge to leap over the table and knock the man flat. He knew the gravity of standing before these men and yet it was anger not fear that seethed dangerously through his muscles. Suddenly the door behind him opened and a woman with a young child came in. She carried a small package. Her dress was brown and worn, the lean years showing in her gaunt cheeks. Her hair, as well as the child's, was wind-swept.

"Bout to storm," she announced.

He lowered his eyes as was expected. As the two men behind the desk turned their attention toward the woman, the anger in him flattened and he seized the moment to slip from the room. The door closed behind him with a thud but no sound of footsteps followed. On another occasion the two men may have been apt to throw Cotton in a cell downstairs until they found out where he'd come from but not today when the tops to their soda bottles had already been removed and Junior had come to pay his daddy a lunchtime visit.

When he stepped outside, the bright day had turned dark and mean. The rain started just as he reached the outskirts of town. An old man pointed him toward a stable where horses were already secured in their stalls. He waited out the short but intense downpour, silent like the animals behind him.

When the rain stopped and the sun popped forth, he set out again to discover a glistening world that wept all around him. Mist hung near the trees and along the rotting wooden fence that marked the road. It kissed the long, stooped grass and the edges of each flowering weed. The rays of sun streamed their light toward the soaked earth. He had never seen such beauty; the brown of a sparrow's feather, the gray of a weathered fence, a black-eyed Susan crushed and floating in a puddle.

"How dare you?" he sighed. The flower just stared with her one eye. "How dare you?"

He did not attempt to register for the draft again, even

after the war began a year later, although he had left the court-house that day determined to do just that. Because of the dripping road, running with every dull and brilliant color he felt he had barely noticed before, he came to the distinct conclusion that he was not to follow a soldier's path. He felt a vague sense of something else tingling under the first layer of his skin. He savored the sensation, carefully positioning it just beyond the edge of a concrete plan so as not to wear it thin nor let it dissolve. When the day came when his father suggested he follow the river north, it then leapt, like a rabbit, into a word Cotton could name. Into his already infamous smile, aspiration spread, bringing forth a sheen one might describe as happiness.

He felt so much himself, so relaxed and unguarded, those last few weeks in Sunset while he prepared for his journey, that he found himself humming as he worked and chatting with his father in a way he had not done before. His father, Luther Lockhart, who held to the notion that an excess of words did not prove advantageous in their town, had become set on one-word answers. But during the weeks prior to Cotton's leaving, the two men often sat up late talking. They speculated as to how long the young peddler, new to these parts, would persist before realizing folks weren't so foolish as to spend their money on something called a sponge.

"Rags is about the only thing we got plenty of," laughed Luther.

They wondered if Roosevelt's New Deal was ever going to crawl all the way down to Arkansas. They spoke respectfully of the president's wife and, while they were still uncertain about the president, they agreed that *she* might actually have a genuine concern for their struggle. They spoke of the war but more so debated the price they would get for their crop this season.

"Regardless, next year will be better," said Cotton. "I'll be sending money down." At that the room hung heavy with thoughts of their separation.

"If you got sense enough to keep your backside from getting froze through," charged Luther to disperse the moment
of gloom. Cotton was leaving at the end of the picking season
so that his absence wouldn't sting so much. It'd be a rough
winter for Luther, where he was sure to go further in the hole,
but Cotton planned to use his northern wages to pull his father, at some point, all the way out.

One evening, his father had gone to visit an aunt over in
the adjacent town of Marion, leaving him alone. He stood in
the open door, the cool autumn air against his bare arms. He
figured the moon, when it came, would rise full. He could already feel its pull deep in the center of his body. Why not, he
decided suddenly. After all this time, why not, just this once?
Just to find out. He set off, grabbing a jacket, and traveling
along a dark road, the soft ground underneath his feet absorbing the sound of his movement. He made it to the small
house near Sutter's Plantation just as the moon rose above
the trees. The young woman inside parted the curtain to see
who was opening the front gate. When she recognized Cotton
she nearly dropped the bowl she was holding. She let go the
curtain, lowered the bowl carefully to the table and closed her
eyes. It was the racket inside her chest that made her realize,
with surprise, that she had been waiting for him.

"I aim to find that cat tonight and bring him in," she
called to her mother in the back room. She lifted her coat
from the hook and slipped outside. He stood at the bottom
of the step with the moonlight behind him just beginning to
spill across the yard.

*

On this cold, moonless November night he reached the
bridge, leaned over the stone ledge and looked down at the
icy river. The water seemed to leap up at the swirling snow
and devour it, then race on ahead. It had been a wet autumn
and it pushed hard and high against the banks, so that even

from where Cotton stood, it was impossible to underestimate its force. If he hopped up and over the ledge the fall would be long, the current would suck him down swiftly. He had no real urge to jump but the probability that it could happen—with him so close and the ledge so easy to hurdle—fooled him into feeling there was part of him considering it.

He took a step back. The snow continued to pile silently around him, diving into the space his feet had just occupied. How strange to be in this wintery place. As often happened, his mind wandered to rest on his father, comparing what each of them might be doing at various present moments, so many miles apart. He had written to his father of his approaching wedding and then had followed with a short note as to why it would never come to be. His father had not responded, merely because Luther did not know how to write and the thought of sending a letter was so foreign that it did not occur to him to ask someone else to transcribe it. Cotton knew this but had hoped, anyway, for a reply.

Along the shore a weak branch, burdened by the snow, broke from its tree and splashed into the water. He imagined it being pulled down under the surface, where objects darker and lonelier waited. Then a movement at the end of the bridge caught his eye. A group of four bodies, two grown and two small, hovered together. One of them seemed to be turned toward him, but it was difficult to discern from such a distance. Did it matter if they spotted him, if they came his way? He recognized that his former habit of dodging trouble seemed to be eroding. Since Hazel's death he was unclear as to what was left to lose from situations that he had so adamantly avoided in the past. In fact, he had started to consider himself a coward for all the years he had spent boxing up his life under the guise of some bigger plan. There was no plan, he now knew, there was just luck. And most of it bad.

Minutes later the family bounded off in the direction they had come. Their dark figures growing smaller as Cotton watched. He felt their absence, an acute loneliness washing over him. If they had not appeared the evening may have stayed intact, but now it was as if a spell had been broken. He looked around to find what moments ago seemed exceptional, sift into mediocrity. The snow grew wet against his clothes, the wind sharper on his face. He stood for a moment longer and then his body decided to begin walking toward home, and yet, when he reached the end of the bridge he did not turn but continued straight, following the path the family had taken. They were out of sight, but the still-falling snow had not yet obscured their tracks.

He found himself traveling up Broadway, the street empty because of the weather. A single car passed as he tromped along the sidewalk. He tugged his hat further over his ears. At one point, he abandoned his dazed pursuit of the four pairs of footprints and was now moving toward the corner where he had lost Hazel.

10

Mary Lang had made a pact with herself, the morning after the streetcar accident when she had been reminded of how fragile life could be, that she would be more faithful in her sisterly duties. Most Saturdays through the fall and now into December she gathered as many of her children as she could, casserole in hand, for a visit to see Uncle Clive. It had been over a year since her mother passed away and her brother now lived alone in the house just a mile north. Even if he did not respond to her visits in the way she hoped, she was determined to see him regularly and Saturdays turned out to be a good day for a brisk walk up.

Before she was married, Mary thought she preferred a life alongside her mother: church every morning, a day full of chores, knitting in the evening. She liked a safe and sure routine that did not allow for the slightest chance that someone could leave one day and never return. When she was ten, her father had left for Duluth on a spring morning and had not, according to a relative who was waiting on his visit, arrived on the day promised, or any day thereafter. He did not leave a trace, except for his old wagon, horse gone, found along a roadside, presents for his sister's children wrapped in brown paper and left on the seat.

Mary's brother, Clive, had been six at the time of their father's disappearance. Now as an adult, he had chosen the life that Mary had thought she wanted. He had lived each day in the house with his mother. He spent most of his time in the room with the mahogany roll top desk calculating figures on paper tablets, discarded envelopes and the backs of grocery lists. He stored the papers in the many slots of the desk, in no particular order it seemed. Yet he could produce, if ever asked, the number of thunderstorms during the summer of '38, the sum of raspberries that had been brought over in a basket from Walter 126 days ago, or the amount of times his mother had cleared her throat on the day she died.

When Mary visited Clive she brought along her youngest children, thinking it would engage his attention. Some days he was more attentive than others. Today, for the first quarter of an hour he conversed like any normal uncle until the bell, too small and close to his ear for anyone else to hear, sounded and his gaze shifted back and forth between his sister's face and the desk and he was forced to get up and go to it.

"I have to, I just have to…" he muttered. "Just this one thing." And in a hurried hand he recorded the combined number of shoelace holes in the children's, his sister's and his own shoes, including the extra pair on the mat near the door. Then he returned to converse with his sister until the bell rang again. After a while Mary announced, to his evident relief, "It's time we get going. Perhaps you'll come down our way for a visit soon?"

"Oh, oh yes," Clive replied but had not, since their mother's death, done so.

On their walk home, they passed Mr. Schneider chopping at patches of ice on his sidewalk. "Hello!" he yelled through the frigid air toward them. "How is everyone?" Mrs. Schneider was at her window behind him, waving. Mary waved back, smiling at the thought of having neighbors that she didn't need to know so well but still felt she could count on.

Frances knew her mother fully expected that her two eldest daughters, since they had not gone along to see Uncle Clive, would have the laundry hanging on the lines in the kitchen well before her return. But Frances had used the morning for her own visiting and so their work had spilled into the afternoon. After the whites they still had a colored batch and then the boy's blue jeans. It would all be dry come morning, she reasoned.

She poured the hot water into the wringer washer as Ethel held a bar of Fels-Naptha over the tub and shaved off a few strips. The water needed to be nearly boiling in order to dissolve the soap. Then they slipped in, one at a time, the clothes from the pile on the floor, watching the electric machine agitate the laundry in a mesmerizing rhythm.

"Will you set my hair while we wait?" Ethel asked, pulling some metal clips and a comb from her apron pocket. "You can just do the front and then I'll wrap a scarf around the rest."

"Okay," Frances said but would have preferred spending a few minutes reading her new book. She combed through a section of Ethel's hair and then wound it around her index finger, pulled her finger out and secured the curl with a clip.

"Joe Mallory asked me to the movies tonight," Frances stated flatly.

"Joe Mallory from church? Bum-knee Joe Mallory? And you didn't tell me until now! Oh gosh, did you say yes?"

"He caught me by surprise when I was coming off the streetcar yesterday and I couldn't think of a good excuse fast enough."

"*Double Indemnity* is still showing. You could see that. How exciting," Ethel hummed.

"Do you think?" asked Frances. "Oh, I know I said he was cute but that seems ages ago. What could we possibly have to talk about? He works at his father's butcher shop and goes to church on Sunday, what else is there to know?"

As Frances secured the last clip and then tied the scarf in a knot at the top of her sister's head, Ethel said, "What's gotten into you? What's so wrong with Joe Mallory, he's just like everybody else around here but more handsome?"

"It's coming through the wringer," Frances pointed. Ethel

grabbed the long stick to stir the clothes as they fell into the rinse water, next they would send them back through the wringer and then hang them on the lines strung across the room.

"You're right," she conceded. "It'll be fun." She tried to sound cheerful, despite finding Ethel's words right on target. Her everyday life and the people in it had grown routine. Since the night of the snowstorm, she preferred to direct her attention toward her rekindled mission to find Hollis, to stay connected in some way to Hazel. Just this morning she had overcome her hesitancy and paid a second visit to Camille Banks. She smiled now, as Ethel's back was turned, with the thought of how pleasant it had turned out.

After the girls had finished the first batch of clothes they began the second, adding hot water from the teakettle to help dissolve the new slice of soap. After the third batch, they hung the last pair of pants and together emptied the tubs of water in the side yard, the discarded water slapping against the icy mounds of snow.

When they were back in the house and had unplugged the washer, pushing it into a corner, Ethel asked, "Are you just staying in then, until evening?"

"Yes, I have a book I want to start."

"You sound more excited about the book than the date."

Frances shrugged. "Did you crush the tin cans or should I get Ray to do it?"

"Definitely Ray, I did fold up all the tinfoil but it's so worn through I can't believe it can be much use to the government or the army or who whoever collects the stuff. Mother must reuse it a half dozen times before she lets it go. She'd probably reuse the tin cans if she could get the lids back on."

The girls laughed. They had been doing their part for the war effort by saving used tin foil and old cans. The gasoline and food rations hadn't really taken a toll on the family, given they didn't own a car and they had never had an excess of sugar from which they could cut back. The girls, with the help of their mother, had taken apart a few old garments and restyled them into new outfits without the need for any new hooks, zippers or snaps, which they would have had trouble getting due to the metal restrictions. It was satisfying to chant "use it up, wear it out, make it do or do without" and, as war-fashion dictated, they had moved their hemline nearly up to the knee. They were both happy to oblige saving material to start a new look, although Ethel complained that she would miss the cuff in men's pants if it disappeared altogether.

Before the war began, things had been much harder. Frances remembered the embarrassment of wearing relief-issued clothes. Everyone knew where the plaid jackets came from and Ethel's silver-rimmed glasses too. The only consolation was that so many other families were also dependent on the handouts of clothes and shoes, given from an empty room in the schoolhouse.

Frances, even though just a child, would lie in bed at night worrying that the electricity would be turned off again. She didn't mind the cozy glow of a candlelit house but even in the dimness it was impossible to miss the frown on her mother's face. She also grew weary of eating so many potatoes and so much oatmeal. She daydreamed about ham and chocolate bars. Her best meals were enjoyed at her grandmother's or Aunt Agnes's house but she did not complain about the soup on Wednesday and Friday. The church had formed a soup society in which the Lang's helped out twice a week, ladling out their own bowls when the long lines dissolved.

She knew that her father's heart was not behind the war despite how their burdens had eased since it began. With the war, Walter had found a steadier flow of tailoring work. There were new and varied opportunities that had not been present before and the newspapers no longer segregated the want ads by gender, needing women to fill positions once reserved for the men now gone off to serve. Mary had even worked for a stretch of time, until her wrists complained too loudly, at the Munsingwear factory making undergarments. The extra income brought fresh fruit, new winter coats and more singing to the house. Yet Frances noticed her father did not share in the patriotic rhetoric that prevailed around them. He was quiet on the subject. Once she found a pamphlet in his trousers, just as she was about to fling them into a soiled laundry pile, written by a group called America First that hoped to keep the country out of the war. She slipped the paper into her father's jacket and never said a word about it.

*

By two o'clock, the clothes had been hung to dry and Ethel was off to the Dime Store. Frances fetched the book Camille Banks had lent her that morning and settled down at the end of the horsehair sofa. The house was unusually quiet and she planned to enjoy it. Walter was delivering a pile of shirts whose collars and cuffs he had repaired during the week. He had three separate houses to call on and would undoubtedly use each as a social visit that, when combined, could span the entire afternoon. He did fine work with his needle and thread. He was not so good at maintaining a steady flow of work nor collecting the money he was owed. Despite intentions of being firm, he was often convinced by each hard luck story that there was a family worse off than his own.

Frances sighed happily into the dreary but peaceful house. The small room was crowded with the sofa, a second-hand piano and a sewing machine. A bolt of fabric leaned against the machine while scraps of cloth spilled from a clothespin bag perched on an old stack of newspapers. The corners of the room, where the linoleum had begun to buckle, held other objects that neither sunlight nor lamplight reached. A gray curtain, hung with wooden loops that slid across a metal pole, partitioned off a front room, which held the beds that the children shared. The kitchen was in the back of the house. The landlord, Walter's second cousin, lived upstairs.

She tucked her feet underneath her and opened the book. As was her habit, she did not turn immediately to the first page, but rather flipped about to get a feel for the book. Near the back she found a section of published letters the author had written to various people. The last letter was dated April 1867. She skipped to the last line. It read: *my love to Miss Daisy. I send her some Jasmine blossoms tell her they bear the fragrance of freedom.* She read the line twice and then ran her thumb along the edge of the pages of the book so that they began to fan out. When the book parted between pages 36 and 37, it fell open. There, thin and nearly transparent, was one sheet of paper folded into thirds. She removed the piece of paper slowly and brought it to her nose. It lacked the scent of blossoms. She unfolded it and began to read:

August 1943
Dear Hazel Banks,
   There is something about me and Cotton you best know. His daddy told me how to reach you, said you two was about to marry. Cotton never loved me and I can't exactly say I did back. But one night he came knocking on my door. No one can rightly claim I'm the kind to get in trouble but some nights ain't meant for the word no and not just because the moon was bright....

Frances lifted her eyes from the paper and imagined, for a moment, a moonlit night and a door upon which to knock. Then she returned to the letter, read the rest of it, and saw the name Ava Morning signed at the bottom. She read it a second time and then just before she was to fold it and slip it back into its spot, she noticed one faint line, added in pencil, a postscript at the very bottom of the page. A line that made her heart lurch. She read it again and again, before finally slipping the letter back into its spot.

11

The first night he came to visit they walked along the path in the forest until they reached the meadow. She then led him by hand to three large rocks along the edge of the clearing from which they could hear the wind in the trees and a faint reminder of the creek flowing further through the woods. The moon cast enough light to see clear across the meadow. No longer holding hands they sat upon separate rocks, the warmth from the day's sun lingering in the smooth, chalky surfaces.

It was not the moonlight; he had lived under its charm forever, nor the stars high above; those too he knew by heart. The late hour, the stillness of the night; these helped, as did the abandoned caution that led him to visit the girl whom he never could push entirely from his thoughts. No, mostly it was Ava's eyes studying his face which convinced him to tell his story and the way she pulled at the words as if they were green tops to the carrots buried below. He began with the news that he'd soon be leaving for life in the north where things were far better and certainly more fair. With that said, the air of impermanence encouraged him to relay to her the details of his life, infused with emotions that had, up until now, been concealed but not at all dismissed. At one point she asked.

"What did your daddy do when your mama died?"

"Carried on. What else could he a done?"

She raised an eyebrow. "Gave up. Could a left somebody else to take care a you." This was the point at which Ava might have introduced her tale of loss. But death and neglect, she wanted to assume, were two different creatures. For her there was still a chance.

Something rustled in the brush behind them, then went quiet. They sat still for a moment listening to the noises of the night. When Cotton spoke again it was nearly a whisper, wanting his voice to blend with the sounds in place. He continued his story, telling her about the green walls of the room inside the courthouse and the two men standing between him and his desire for military service. He told her of the rainstorm, the drooping flowers and their dazzling assurance that there was more for him than life in a uniform.

He looked out over the silvery grass and said, "Before I go I'd like to draw this meadow." Then he turned to her, "Thank you for letting me bend your ear, Ava Morning."

They walked back toward the house. Just before they stepped from the shelter of the trees and into the open space around the house, she stopped. She so wanted to ask her sister May what she should do. While her sister had gone and left awhile back, Ava had never shook the habit of seeking her advice. She wanted to ask her what she should say, how she might hold onto him a little longer. The answer was silent and clear. No one could lengthen the span of a minute, or stretch anything more from an hour. She could not turn a chance at love into love. She would not mistake the two.

She stood in front of Cotton, their bodies close. She looked up toward the sky, the tops of the trees swaying against midnight, and then back to his face. "You go on and have you a good life," she whispered, putting a finger to her lips so he wouldn't respond and then she spun slowly away from him. She resolved to prevent this night from chasing after the empty days that would follow. She was already lonely before he came, she reminded May, his leaving wouldn't change a thing.

She began to step into the long grass that led to the house when they heard a stick crack under the weight of something heavy. Twenty yards to the left, at the edge of the woods stood a woman dressed in a long, white nightgown.

"Mama?" Ava called.

Josetta Morning, in a raspy voice called back, "Did you see 'em?" She then crept forward on bare feet, her head uncovered so that the moon traveled like rivers along the gray streaks in her hair.

The story, as Ava had come to learn it, was that Josetta's father had been sent off to a neighboring farm, having owed on a debt he couldn't find any other way to pay off. Josetta, then five, was assured that her father would one day come back. She waited, looking in the direction she imagined him returning.

She now spoke to her grown daughter, "Papa said he'd be back 'fore the cold rain come again. Said stir the pot with a long handle so you ain't like to catch your sleeve on the flame. Be back 'fore them eggs take to hatchin'. Don't let it peck your tiny hand, Shoo Fly. See, took to call me Shoo Fly cause I stick close when he around. Yes, be coming now 'fore the tears dry them cheeks up to salt. Don't worry none hear, Lil' Shoo Fly."

Ava could not remember her mama stringing together multiple sentences, coherent or not, in years. To hear the words of a child coming from a grown woman broke the daughter apart. A thousand tiny pieces of Ava fell to the ground in front of her mother.

"Oh, mama. He can't come back. He just can't. He tried, I know he must a tried till he couldn't try no more."

Josetta looked at her child, "Till he couldn't try no more?"

"Something must a kept him from getting to you. Had to be," said Ava.

Josetta continued to stare at Ava. Her papa had been hung from a poplar tree for what reason no healthy being could imagine. She had been sheltered from this news and yet still she knew of it; conversation not meant for her ears, a pack of crows gathered along the fence, winter in her mother's eyes. Such things a young girl might choose to ignore, then bury, in an attempt to cling to the hope of a daddy's return.

"I best think on that," Josetta said at last. But she already had. After years of forgetting, in one instant she remembered. Cotton grabbed Josetta's arm as she began to sway. She leaned into him and then jumped back as if startled to realize she was not alone.

"Who's that?"

"Cotton, ma'am, they call me Cotton. Let me help you to the house."

"Cotton," her voice melted, as if the name by itself made sense.

He walked her back to the house, looking once over at her daughter whose face was lowered toward the ground. After Ava had gotten her mama in bed, she peered out the window to see Cotton closing the gate.

The following morning Josetta did not get out of bed. While this was not unusual, the crying and moaning made Ava boil her mother an egg and add extra honey to the tea. Each time Ava entered the room the moaning grew louder until Ava kept herself in the kitchen and then out in the yard near the wood-pile. She tried to worry about her mama but the old habit was overrun by thoughts of Cotton. She sighed, wishing to have gotten close enough to catch the scent of his skin.

She decided he would not be back. After all, she had bid him a good life and, moreover, who wouldn't be spooked by the antics of her mother? She bent to pick up chunks of wood that had previously been cut but never stacked. She stayed squatting, her back warmed by the October sun, while she thought of his strong hand, rough but warm, holding her own. She recalled both the glimmer in his eye as he relayed his plans and the pinch around his mouth from disappointments of the past. She stayed longest in the moments of his smile, when it had spread over her like the moon in the meadow, when it had convinced her mama to lean against his arm.

"I told you he was something," she said to May.

Indeed, came the reply.

Ava stood up with a cord of wood in each hand that she added to the stack against the shed. She bent again for more and continued in this way until the area was cleared of all but a number of the good-sized branches of an old tree that had fallen last month, still needing to be sectioned and cut to fit the grate of the fireplace. The effort it took to lug over a single one to the cutting stump turned her breathing jagged. She paused to look out across the yard. By the light the sun cast across the stone path leading up to the house and through the feathery growth of the evergreen near the gate, she knew it was long past lunchtime. She needed to get inside and fix something, although she doubted it would be eaten. Perhaps just a warm helping of baked fruit would suffice. She would need the butter she had churned a few days back. A few sticks of it remained, keeping cool in the pail near the bottom of the well. She would walk out to the hill and pull up the pail, after she picked the apples.

From the tree in the back she plucked ten sour apples from the lowest branches. Tomorrow she would find a ladder to harvest the bounty beyond her reach, turning some into pies but most into jelly that would last through the winter. She stood near the trunk, and looking upward through the maze of fluttering green leaves and the web of brown bark she spotted blue diamonds of sky.

A few hours later, as she pulled a steaming pot from the wood-burning oven, lunch preparations having spilled into dinner, it occurred to her that she had been ignoring a dull but repetitive thwacking sound coming from the yard. She set the baked apples topped with cinnamon sugar and oatmeal on the table, before walking out to the porch. The axe was raised high in the air and then brought down with enough force to split the wood clean and make it bounce up for Cotton's left hand to catch. He had finished all but a few logs scattered at his feet. He did not hear her behind him. The sun was still warm but it was dropping as she continued to watch. She was amazed at how reassuring it felt to have him in the yard. After a while he placed the blade of the axe in the cutting stump's well-worn gash and turned around.

Ava was tempted to call out that it wasn't right to sneak around people's property and nothing but foolish to then let them take you by surprise, but a weight at the base of her tongue kept her from talking. Cotton walked forward, wiping the sweat off his brow with a sleeve. He wanted to tease her about paying him with apple pie for the cut wood—the aroma had reached out into the yard—but it did not seem a time for words. What had formed between them last night now settled in the hollow of the coming evening, scattering conversation into the day before. Shadows had begun to lengthen softly from their objects and stillness gathered just below the branches of the trees. Cotton had tried not to notice the things he might one day miss, and yet here he was again in front of Ava Morning.

"Hungry?" she asked. He nodded.

They ate the warm apples around the kitchen table, Josetta finally getting out of bed when Ava told her Cotton had come to pay her a visit. She sat at the table watching him, occasionally spooning the food to her mouth. When the meal was over she stood up, clutching the sweater around her shoulders, and thanked him for the visit. She then went out on the front porch to sit in her rocking chair.

"Screen on the front door needs mending," Josetta called in a few minutes later. Ava's mouth dropped open, having thought the roof needed to cave in to draw a comment from her mother regarding the condition of anything around the place. She had just cleared the plates from the table. Cotton smiled and called out, "Yes, ma'am. I was just getting to that."

Ava giggled and pointed under the sink to where she kept a few spare tools in an old coffee tin. Cotton went to work on the door, feeling Josetta watching him from her rocker. Today he had left the field early, giving his bag to the strawboss to weigh without saying a word. Picking season had begun in August and now in October they were on the top crop where the bolls were often underdeveloped and the yield of lesser quality than the earlier crops. He didn't expect the man to question him since his sack was already, by four, as heavy as what anyone else would bring in by six. He was paid his week's wage, the strawboss hesitant to challenge his best worker—having no idea that Cotton would not be back Monday morning or any morning thereafter—and only watched with irritation as the young man sauntered off as if there was someplace to go.

Cotton was cautious not to break the brittle frame of the door, prying it off carefully so that he could stretch the fraying screen out to the edges. He hammered the wood back in place and returned the tools. Both women were on the porch now.

"There's a couple holes I couldn't much do anything about. But the screen's tight again, ma'am."

She nodded, letting the chair go still. She caught his gaze in her own before she spoke.

"You fixin' to make my sweetest one happy." Was it a question or a statement? He couldn't be sure. "Go on you two," she said. "Moon be up soon."

Ava took her mama's words and held them tight within her clenched fist, then followed Cotton into the yard. They took the road for a while until angling off down a well-worn path that led to the water. By the time they reached the edge of the creek the moon hung orange and heavy through the trees. It was dark as she bent down to open her hand to the water, dipping it all the way under and letting the current run through it. When she stood up, he was close behind. He turned her around, leaving his hand on the small of her back. The space between them, slim like a piece of paper carrying on it the day's unspoken words, held for a moment before being crushed. As he brought her down onto the soft sand, knowing she was her mama's sweetest one, she brought her nose against the fabric of his shirt and inhaled. She did not think to ask May a single question until an hour later, when they both lay quietly on their backs, the moon now white and assuming up above.

12

Lewis Banks welcomed the cold weather. He encouraged the hard bite of the wind against his forehead. He stood on the train's platform and drew his breath in through his mouth, letting it rip at his lungs. The high peaked roof did nothing on a blustery day in early December, to prevent the wind from howling across the open-sided station. The cold sliced through his pant legs and long underwear, tearing at his shins. It bore through his wool cap, and against the tender skin of each eardrum. Lewis hoped the brittle air might clear away the sorrow that hung like a heavy cape around his neck.

As passengers stepped from the train, he listened to them bemoan the afternoon, reluctant suddenly to replace their stuffy boxcars for a bitter wind. He worked steadily, distributing the luggage to its appropriate rider, while impatient feet stomped around him. Their breathing, throaty and visible, reminded him of a team of restless horses. Off to his left he could hear a man's pocket watch clicking open and closed.

In the past he had resisted the onslaught of winter. Never, in the eighteen-year process of adapting to Minnesota, had he grown accustomed to the abrupt arrival of the first frost and, then worse, the long months to follow. Until this year, he much preferred the slow pattern of warm days and thick nights. Mid-summer was his favorite, when he waited on nightfall to carry the songs of crickets and bullfrogs, the owl hunting its prey, insects tunneling into the cool earth. On still nights, after Camille and Hazel had fallen asleep, he had stood on the back porch listening across the long, rectangular backyard and through the wooded stand of trees until he could, with effort, detect the sound of water. It forced him along through the tangled path of brush and moonlight until he came to the creek moving mildly in its bed, pooling in pockets close to shore. He removed his shoes and socks to let the water seep between his toes. He closed his eyes waiting for expectation to steam up from the dark earth around him, the sound of it filling what had been drained away by life's daily demands. He smiled to be part of the night's music.

When Lewis was young, he spent his summer days bent over rows of vegetables alongside his younger sister Ivy. They worked in silence. When an occasional word was exchanged—to determine the time to break for lunch or whose turn to fill the water pail—it seemed out of place among the natural noises around them. The steep climb of the mountain behind and the large plot of land, almost too big to be called a garden, demanded his full attention. He used his ears far more than his eyes to pay attention. They worked until the sun was high above, then they rested and played in the shade of the woods and in the trickle of the stream. By late afternoon, when they spotted their mother coming up the road with her basket emptied of the produce she had distributed among their neighbors on her way to cook for Miss Nancy, they rushed to meet her. Ivy, by then, had a barrage of stored words to unleash.

Lewis added his fair share of comments, saving the best details for when their father arrived, overalls soiled and dusted from the work he did on Mr. Down-in-the-Mouth's farm. Mr. Down-in-the-Mouth owned all the land from where they lived out to the main road, which seemed like most of the world to Lewis but in fact wasn't but 50 acres. Mr. Down-in-the-Mouth went by another name to all but the Banks family who hoped, as they sat at the table enjoying the evening meal, that he would continue to ignore the dilapidated and weed-infested spot he rented to them. Surely he would demand more money if he saw how the enormous garden flourished and the cabin, too small to be a house, leaned a little to the left with happiness.

Lewis relayed the activities of the day. Another anthill had appeared at the end of the strawberries. The skunk family had settled into a birch tree rotting near the fence. Throughout the morning, three ruby-throated hummingbirds hovered near the flowering pumpkin patch.

"I didn't see none a that," Ivy complained.

"Neither did I," replied Lewis. "I heard it."

His father turned to his mother and said, "That boy could hear a tomato burp."

The house remained noisy until exhaustion drained the laughter out of each of their four bodies. Lewis listened to the whip-poor-will's goodnight call, the sun just gone, for at least a full minute before he fell into a deep sleep that only the rooster could disturb.

Eventually Mr. Down-in-the-Mouth did wander down their dead end road and level the claim that field hands could not appreciate such choice land. Within a year he had the cabin converted into a shed and a new house built close by. The new house was awkward and cold, the shadow of the mountain seeming to follow it regardless of the time of day. The weeds came back to overtake the garden by the time the Banks, with nowhere else to go, had left the foothills of the Allegheny Mountains and journeyed further east through West Virginia in hopes of finding work in the city.

Lewis turned twelve as the old century slipped into the new. When they stalled in a town called Malden, just before Charleston, he watched his father's spirit wane with each daily, coal-shoveling trip into the drift mine.

"Ain't the worst job. Ain't me whose inside, stuck to blast the coal loose. In and out with my cart, I still see the sun," John Banks told his boy. Then his face grew stiff. "Even so, you ain't never going in. That, I'm a see to."

So John sent his children to the little school that had been started by a light-skinned man from Ohio just after the end of the Civil War. A man who had taught the young by day and the old by night, most all newly freed and bent on learning just how twenty-six letters could begin to make sense when put to paper. The one room schoolhouse, occupied by Booker T. Washington for a short time, survived the thirty-five years it took for Lewis to take a seat near the wall by the windows. To please his father, he applied himself to his studies, despite being distracted by a skinny girl named Camille who sat under the nose of the teacher. He kept his eyes focused on his work but he listened for every thump and rustle coming from her direction.

Since arriving in the crowded, smelly place, he ached for the peace and laughter that no longer came as easily to him and his family. The skinny girl who rarely smiled, aroused a sense of wonder that reminded him of the chicory that grew wild and resilient back home. Was chicory—or blue sailors as they preferred to call it—the color of the sky or rather the sky the color of the flowering plant? Lewis wondered if Camille, sitting so attentively at the front of the room with her sky blue answers, was the color of his current life or the one that had yet to begin?

Twenty years later, and not a day of it spent in the darkness of a coal mine, it took the arrival of his daughter Hazel to convince him that a grubby little city, or a flat cold one, shared the same sky as a fertile field, too big to be called a garden. Before going north to Minnesota, though it was hours out of the way, he rode his family back to the foothills of the mountains. He found the spot. A dying, abandoned house sunk into the earth behind the tiny cabin. The field, his field, was awash in yellow foxglove, orange milkweed and the purple-black berries ripe on the pokeweed stalks. The blue of the chicory led him to what was once the pumpkin patch. There among weed stems and flower blossoms and the lush smell of earth, one green squash grew on a gnarled vine. He thought to pick it for Hazel but then decided no. The meat would eventually rot and its seeds press into the ground and start anew. As they rode off, he resolved to indulge in the sprawling nature of pumpkin plants when they reached Minnesota, regardless of the size and shape of their new backyard.

When they arrived, for the first three weeks they kept a room at the Phyllis Wheatley House. It was cramped and gloomy but they did not utter a word against the charity offered them. Camille, Lewis noted, seemed withdrawn. She'll adjust, he had told himself. And then at the end of the third week, he landed a job at the Minneapolis Athletic Club where twenty-nine other black employees already worked. He knew nothing about operating an elevator but the manager had mistaken his quiet demeanor and physical height for competency and he had opted not to argue the point. The position allowed the family to move from the settlement house to the top floor of a duplex where Hazel could run across the hardwood floors, annoying the tenants below. Camille brightened and spent her days with the little girl in the high, sunny kitchen baking sweet breads that they would then nibble on in the backyard atop an old blanket. An extra loaf was given to the downstairs neighbors, which allowed for the noisy running to continue.

Yet, the enthusiasm that had once echoed in Camille's voice, particularly upon arriving home from her adventures as a schoolteacher, was missing in their new home. This did not go undetected by Lewis. He clung to the hope that she would find a new teaching position. His mistake, and hers as well, was that they left this hope silent between them until it turned into something they no longer recognized. Even after he landed a coveted union position with the railroad and she had begun her ironing work for the laundry company, he continued his silent communion with her disappointment, thinking she would interpret it as support.

Not once did she level a complaint against their new life. Compared to their neighbors they had fared well and Hazel was flourishing in school. They soon came to own their own home, with a porch and a garden, and two steady incomes they could count on. Still he knew of the nodule of bitterness inside his wife that, in difficult moments, fought to make itself known.

*

Life goes by in a minute, Lewis thought, as he reached for the handle of a woman's suitcase, careful not to touch her gloved fingers. He bent his knees as he lifted the luggage, anticipating the muscles of his lower back to complain. He had not slept well since Hazel's death and he could feel it in his aging body. He had seen to the emptying of the train an hour earlier and was now helping to send off the next group of travelers. He was thankful, after a five-day shift, that for him this was the end of the line. When the last of the passengers had boarded and the platform was clear, the train pulled out. He raised his hand in response to the hiss of the engine. The train eased away and he was left alone under the iron rafters of the lonely, frigid station. Along the wall was a row of employee lockers. He opened his to pull out rubber boots for the walk home, the first snow of the season having fallen while he had been away. Between the boots lay a note. It had been dropped through a slit at the top of the locker. It read: *I have found the truck. Belongs to a man out west of the city. When the roads clear I could go.*

After the police had closed the case, Lewis had hired a private detective. This note meant the detective found someone to identify the truck and now had tracked down the owner. He folded the note and thrust it deep into his pocket. His heart raced. He left the station, charging out into the afternoon where the snow was piled along the sidewalks. When he stepped out among the pedestrians, the sun broke through the clouds. It occurred to him, as the slant of sunshine hit his shoulder just right, that the thought of Camille, and only Camille, waiting for him at home, might one day come to be enough. With this, he buttoned the top of his coat collar and began his journey.

✳

On the Saturday morning Frances was to discover the letter, twice she rapped her gloved knuckles against the Banks' door before the glint of the doorbell caught her eye. She frowned at her oversight, pressed the round button and waited. She wanted this visit to be a good idea, ignoring the voice within her arguing that she should have gone with the others to Uncle Clive's instead.

Camille was at her ironing board in the kitchen, trying to envision what canned vegetables remained on the shelves behind the closed cupboard doors. Lewis would be returning later in the day—from what seemed to her an endlessly long stretch—but she had not yet mustered the desire to prepare him a decent meal. When the doorbell rang, the iron gave a slight jerk in her hand. She returned it to its metal tray and went to the door, spotting Frances through the sheer curtain. As of late, visitors were something she had come to dread but the sight of the girl gave her heart a moment's lift. She had been hoping for this return visit. As she greeted Frances she noted how foreign her own voice sounded, not having used it during her husband's absence.

"I hope you don't mind that I've stopped for a visit," Frances began, "I would understand entirely if you didn't feel up to seeing me. I could even come at a better time."

"No, please come in."

They settled in the front room, where sunlight fell softly through the windows and onto the furniture. While Camille left for the kitchen to make tea, Frances looked around, latching onto the patterns in the wallpaper and then the rug at her feet. She let the stillness of the room surround her, engulf her, slowing her thoughts until she was no longer chasing after what had already happened and what was yet to come.

"What a lovely room. I could spend all day reading on this sofa," she spoke, her words ticking like the clock on the mantle, when Camille returned with a tray in hand.

"That's just what Hazel would do on sunny, winter days." Camille set the tray on the table. "She loved her books. I guess I spoiled her some because I preferred to let her read rather than call for her help with chores." She poured the strong black tea into each cup and added cream. She stirred with a small spoon as Frances watched the liquid swirl, a waft of steam lifting from each cup. "She never was any good with work around the house, but lord knows she was smart as a whip." She had not discussed her daughter in any detail since her death, even with Lewis. But somehow the warmth of the room and the listener, who seemed to be sent for such a purpose, encouraged her to continue. "She was to begin teaching this fall. That Monday she would have entered the classroom. It was my dream, and of course her dream as well, that she would teach. I wanted her to see the children's faces light up when she praised them. That's the best part, when they beam." The cup and saucer rattled softly in her hand as she passed it to Frances. "She would have made a fine teacher, too. She was bright and had such enthusiasm, quoting to me from what she was reading, as if I'd not read the books myself. In fact, just that morning she had convinced me to take down some old boxes that I'd been storing in the attic. She couldn't understand why I'd kept them from her. To tell the truth, I had forgotten I'd packed away more than just school books." She stared into her tea before taking a sip. "She would have gotten to every last one, I'm sure of it. Turns out she had barely time to open one. They're all still up there, right where she left them. I haven't gone in that room but to dust."

The sunlight stretched toward the footstool in front of an empty chair.

"Do you like to read, Frances? Now Mr. Banks he prefers the radio but my daughter and I, well, we really enjoyed ourselves a good book."

"Why yes, I certainly do. Although I can't seem to find many new ones on the shelves at the public library."

"You mean within that whole big building there is nothing you haven't read?"

Frances laughed, "Oh, gosh no. That's not what I meant. In the section I like they don't seem to want to order too many new ones."

"And what section would that be?'

"Oh, I prefer fiction. I have to admit I like a mystery, or best of all, a love story."

Camille, finished with her tea, stood up and beckoned Frances to follow. "I bet I can find you a story you may like. Come with me, we have to go upstairs."

She followed Camille up the staircase, marveling at how receptive, compared to last time, the woman was acting. She would never have predicted sharing such comfortable conversation. It was a relief and yet the topic she had come to discuss had yet to be mentioned.

They entered a small room with half-emptied boxes and untidy piles of books scattered across a green, braided rug. The bookshelf stood bare. Camille looked down at the boxes for a moment, contemplating a course of action for finding the book she had in mind. She thought some poetry by Paul Laurence Dunbar might lead Frances to an interest in something beyond fiction. But where to find it?

"What's this?" Frances cried bending over a book that was splayed open with its cover aimed toward the ceiling. "*Incidents in the Life of a Slave Girl,*" she read out loud.

She studied the photo of the author, an elderly woman with white hair sitting in an ornate, high-backed chair. The woman had her hands folded in her lap and wore a smile. She turned to Camille and commented, "She doesn't look anything like a slave."

"How do you mean?"

"Well, first off, she looks close to being white."

"Close has never counted, I'm afraid."

"Well, besides that," Frances rushed ahead, "she looks so dignified. I mean she's nicely dressed and her face looks, well, happy."

Camille took a moment to look at the image. "It is hard to imagine much happiness within slavery, but I think they managed a little. People are always bigger than their circumstance and no one, I would argue, *looks* like a slave. That would be our imagination trying to make sense of a ridiculous arrangement."

"I'm sorry Mrs. Banks. I didn't mean to be out of line."

"No need, child," said Camille, "In fact, I agree she does look happy. I believe by the time the photograph was taken, she had gained her freedom. I was going to suggest a different book but perhaps you'd like that one. While it's nonfiction I bet you might find a hint of love in it."

Frances stared again at the cover of the book. "I'd love to borrow it. If you're sure it's alright."

Camille nodded. Then she looked at the rest of the books strewn about the room. She knew they needed to be shelved but she could not imagine being the one to do it. She watched the young woman pick up another book and turn it over in her hand.

"You sure have a lot of books. Would it help it I set them on a shelf after I peeked at the titles?" asked Frances, like she was offering to put the cover on the butter dish.

Camille nodded again and moved to the window, wrapping her shawl tighter around her shoulders. She did not want to lose this reminder of Hazel but she also sensed that the disarray of the room inhibited her and her husband. They needed to be able to pass by without avoiding a glance in. And she still had Hazel's bedroom to savor.

A quiet hour later Frances had all but one box of books shelved. She stood up rather abruptly, Camille who was dusting the woodwork around the windows, looked over.

"I've let the time get away. I really need to get home, my mother is expecting me."

"Of course. Thank you for your help and don't forget your book. When you've finished it, you're welcome to come back for another."

"Oh thank you, and I must return to shelve the last box."

Frances was baffled that two hours could slip by without moving anywhere close to the conversation for which she had come, without being able to ask any more questions about Hazel's dying request. By the weary look on the older woman's face she didn't feel it right to try now. She would come back.

"How is Cotton doing?" she asked as she was leaving out the front door of the house.

Camille pointed and said only, "He stays there at Miss Emma's place."

By the time she was half way home, book in hand and letter hidden within, Lewis Banks was walking into a house that greeted him with only the aroma of canned soup and the fading smell of a hot iron. In place of a decent meal his wife shared with him one long embrace and the finer details of Frances's two visits. Lewis only listened; he was not ready to share his own news. There was not enough of it, yet.

13

Grandmother had lived along the banks of the lower Minnesota River for much of her 94 years. This area was named after Chief Sakpe and was now called Shakopee. She had left when she was a girl and hadn't returned until she was a young woman. She did not talk much about the years she was gone. They were not ones easy to retell yet they were not ones she could forget, even now.

She had been twelve in 1862 when her people had risen up against the United States government. The Dakota Conflict they called it, as if it were nothing more than a dispute over the price of butter and not the tragic culmination of stolen land and broken treaties, starving people who were told by the white agency that owed them money "to eat grass." After a month of fighting, in which hundreds of white civilians were killed, the warriors were defeated, caught like rabbits by a wolf. Thirty-eight Indian men were sent to hang in Mankato, her father among them. Afterward all Dakota were forced to leave the state, even those who had not participated in the fighting. She and her mother, along with so many other women and children, were loaded on steamboats and shipped down the Mississippi. Later they were sent west along the Missouri River to Crow Creek.

Crow Creek turned out to be a place so desolate and barren that her heart sank as they filed off the boat and walked across the wind-swept, snow-covered land. Her mother squeezed her hand to remind her of the ones who had died along the way. So many had not survived the first walk, when they had been herded away from their land into Fort Snelling. Nor the cold winter they spent huddled there with little food and disease all around. And more died, too many to count, as they journeyed along the rivers, the boats over-crowded. When they arrived at Crow Creek she was devastated, having clung to the thought of a destination to keep her from losing all hope when so much misery surrounded her. But she recognized instantly that this was no place to hope to arrive. She looked around for the trees. They were missing, along with the men.

Her mother decided that her daughter must have a reason to get up each morning so she gave her the responsibility of helping with the little ones, some having lost their mothers already. She stayed with them even when they grew listless from hunger, even when they lay crying from sickness. And especially when they stopped crying, that was when she knew they would not last long. "You must do this," her mother told her in Santee. "Even if it brings tears. Tears are the medicine."

There was never enough food. The soldiers told them to boil the green berries from the cottonwood trees, so she collected them from the few stands of trees surrounding the camp. Then she put them in a pot over the fire. When she fed them to the others, they held their stomachs and groaned until they wretched the soup back up. Finally, the white missionary who had traveled by boat with them, convinced a colonel to let the few Dakota men in the camp go on a buffalo hunt. They ate better the winter of '63 but after that the hunger came back.

When her mother died, they had been at the camp for three years. Her mother had been the one to go to the horse corrals in the morning and pick the grain out of the horses' feces, to take back and feed to the children. At first she could not bring herself to go to the stables and take over her mother's task, but eventually she found it was the only thing to do. Her mother had been right, she had to find a reason to get up each morning. She thought of her father and how he had died; she thought of her mother, how she wasted away so that her daughter would not. She vowed, as she looked out upon the vast, desolate land that did not feel familiar, to make her way back to the river and to the trees that knew how to whisper her name.

And she did. She came back in the late 1880's as a woman with a husband and two children beside her. By then, Chief Shakopee and Little Crow had been executed and there were only a handful of people she knew that remained. But the trees, the stream, the river were the same. She stood on the riverbank and felt her feet touch the earth. She felt her breath touch the sky. For all the mothers and fathers who had lost their daughters, she became the daughter. For all the daughters and sons who had lost their mother, she eventually became the mother.

Now that she was old, she thought back on those she had held on to and those that had slipped through. Her eldest son, who was now called Uncle Lee, had married a woman with light eyes and thought it better that their children know the ways of city life. He rarely returned to visit, but without fail, each month sent back a few dollars with Chayton. Money Grandmother silently slid into a drawer. Money they desperately needed but that she would have traded in an instant for the one that had been named Chaska so long ago, he being the first son. As a young boy he came to earn the name Little Thunder because of his strength and determination. Then he was taken to the mandatory boarding school and his name was changed to Lee Smith. When he returned from the school, Little Thunder was gone, only a boy with a white name remained.

In place of one son, she clung to others, especially Chayton her great-grandson. Especially him. There was something about him that flattened her heart and then filled it back up.

✱

Ava Morning's grandfather had been six when the Civil War ended and the owners of the Sutter plantation abandoned it. The women and children of the Sutter family, giving up on the hope that their men would return from the war and restore normalcy, fled one fearful night when the cellar had run bare and their slaves had taken to looking them dead in the eye. Out of those unappreciated people who had carried the physical burden of the plantation; who had maintained the crops, the animals, the house, and attended to the slaveholder's every demand, from urgently vital to annoyingly trivial; out of those, a cluster chose to stay. For a few months they quietly prospered off the land, working hard but eating well, resting in the evenings, singing to their children, worshiping on Sunday. Most didn't believe such good fortune would last, looking down the road for a sign of bad luck, listening at dusk for the sound of discord.

In the end someone with a tall hat and a northern accent stumbled across the Sutter plantation, outside the small town of Sunset, Arkansas. He put a stop to the tranquility, tracking down Mrs. Sutter's second cousin from St. Louis who jumped at the chance to chain the people to the land in a new way. As tenant farmers the former slaves, regardless of how hard they worked or how well they planned for a successful harvest, gradually fell into a debt from which climbing out was nearly impossible.

When Ava's grandfather turned fourteen he decided to set off, telling his mama he'd look around for something better and then come back for her. He was young enough not to recognize that his absence would require the others to work harder and longer, a sacrifice they were willing to make because his departure resembled independence, which they needed to believe was possible for some of them, somewhere.

First thing he did was drop the name Sutter, not that he had ever used it, but being a former slave of the Sutter plantation it was the closest thing he had to a sir name. To drop it simply meant to choose another. It was a beautiful spring morning as he walked along the dirt road leading out of Sunset, and the birds called to each other with such excitement that he stopped to listen. They seemed so intent on discussing his well-being, so happy that he was walking toward a better place. A birdsong never sounded as pure as it did in the morning, when the prospect for the day was still golden.

"Morning," he said aloud, willing the rest of his life to hold such promise. And he took the name.

Unfortunately, after fifteen years of moving from one southern town to the next, he arrived back at the Sutter Place with but a few extra dollars in his pocket. The length of his absence and the charm of the half-true stories he had a knack for telling, made it easy to make the new name stick. He soon passed it along to his son and his son's children, until it reached a baby girl who went by the first name of Ava.

By the time Ava was born in 1923, there were already six sisters in front of her. When she came out, her mama said to her daddy, "You gonna have to find you somebody else to get you that boy."

Ava struggled to win an adequate amount of her mother's attention. It was not that Josetta Morning was an uncaring mother, it was that her responsibilities pressed too heavily upon her. There was the string of endless requests spouting from mouths always hungry, clothes needing mending, hair needing plaiting. She nursed and bathed the new baby, tried to jabber and snuggle with her, but it was an effort that grew increasingly challenging. It was as if the one before Ava had taken the last drop, leaving nothing in the way of patience or affection for Josetta to give. She stayed longer and longer within the space of her mind that was blank, seldom speaking and partaking only in duties that required a physical presence and nothing more until, eventually, her afternoons spent on the front porch staring into the woods, as if she was expecting someone to emerge, began to stretch past sundown. Her oldest daughters had no choice but to take over.

For Ava, there was Tula and May. Tula, second to the oldest, picked Ava out of her mother's arms one morning and never really gave her back, except to feed. Tula wrapped Ava in a cloth and tied the baby onto her back while she worked. Ava, belly down, could feel her sister's heartbeat like a steady, slower second of her own. In the evenings, Tula, at thirteen, bathed her sister with a damp cloth and called to May, just five, to sing so the baby wouldn't fuss.

As Ava grew from baby to child, her mother continued to fade in and out on her family. The girls' daddy did his best to put food on the table by working the same fields his family had worked for so far back it became too burdensome to remember. Tula continued to take special care of Ava's needs, while May came to be her confidant, her best source of entertainment and a bubbling spring of true and false information.

"What makes night crawlers gooey?" Ava would ask.

"They slither in your nose when you sleep and steal your snot," replied May.

"How come boys wear pants instead of dresses?"

"They ain't learnt how to pee yet," answered May.

"Why do I dream about mama every night?"

"Cause she won't let you forget her. She crawls in through your eye while god has your soul. Don't you know, God takes your soul at night and gives it back in the morning?"

"Lots a stuff crawls in at night," said Ava. "Can't God just leave mama in there?"

"No," barked May, "mama needs to watch the woods so she can spot her papa coming home from the other plantation."

"What other one?" Ava had started to cry.

"The one they sent him to when mama was only nine, same age as me. That's why mama can't think 'bout nothing else but how to get grandpapa back. Don't cry now, it'll make the worms come."

✳

While she was young she followed Tula around the kitchen, dipping her finger in batter and hiding eggs in her apron pockets. She preferred to play under the table with the rolling pin or count the cooking pots hanging from the ceiling rather than join the other children in their games outside. As she grew, she became increasingly helpful to her sisters so that by ten she was happily responsible for a good portion of the daily cooking. She especially enjoyed baking. She liked to give her daddy hot biscuits in the morning and if there was extra flour in the bin and fruit to pick from the yard, a pie on Sunday. She always set down a slice in front of her mother, who ignored it, to Ava's repeated disappointment.

Tula waited as long as she could before getting married. She waited until May was old enough to take care of both mama and Ava, not that the other sisters couldn't do it, but May still whispered encouragement in her mama's ear and sang her little sister to sleep every night. Yet one day it was time for May to leave as well.

"You see I just gotta go. You'll understand when your own man comes along. I'm aching to see the world, girl, and he's got a big shiny car to take us all the way to New Orleans." May's voice slipped into its familiar tone and she continued, "It's true, no one sleeps in that town. You get you one a them witch doctors to hang a glass bottle on a tree outside and you don't never feel tired."

She leaned the broom she had been sweeping with against the wall and put a hand on Ava's cheek. "Tula's straight down the road. She'll help with mama till I get back."

After May was gone, the house filled with silence. Only Ava and her mother were left, the other sisters having scattered to begin their own grown-up lives and their father already two years in the grave from a life worn out. Tula tried to walk over every day so that Ava had an opportunity to engage in a two-way conversation. The sisters sat in the kitchen talking, a baby on one lap and a bowl of something needing to be stirred on the other.

She kept baking and soon developed a reputation, especially for her cakes. It began with her sisters' weddings and spiraled outward until she was baking a cake for nearly everyone getting married in and around Sunset. She met Cotton one Sunday afternoon in the churchyard as she stood behind a table placing increasingly thinner slices of wedding cake onto mismatched plates. She hoped her payment this time might be money, although she expected it would be another live chicken or a few bottles of milk. The depression had recently ended, but people in Sunset were still waiting for things to get better.

Camped under the shade of a pine tree, Cotton watched patiently as the line for cake came to an end. Just as a near-by circle of children took up another song, he approached her table. She had given out the last of the cake moments before, relieved that everyone had gotten a piece. When he arrived she frowned at him. He looked down at the table, bare but for crumbs, an empty serving plate and a few forks.

"Looks to me I'm out a luck," he said.

She knew of Cotton. The one so many girls had a crush on and yet it was said that he showed no interest in anyone. Why is he talking to me, she would have liked to have asked May? *'Cause he likes cake,* came May's reply, *and you might be half-cute if you dust off some of that sugar and flour.*

"*Half*-cute?" Ava said out loud.

"Pardon?"

"Oh… nothing," she giggled, waving one hand. "It's just a habit. I reckon I used to ask my sister just about every question under the sun and now, sometimes, it seems like she's still trying to get in an answer."

"You gotta a sister here who thinks I might be half-cute?" he said looking over his shoulder. He surprised himself with such a frivolous comment, knowing there was nothing to gain from it. He found himself staring at her the way one might sit up in bed straining in the dark to identify a pair of overalls hanging from a hook on the wall. He had seen her plenty of times, knew she was from a family of which there were too many girls to keep straight, yet suddenly she appeared fascinating. Was there something he was supposed to know about her that made this moment seem more important than all the ones before, that infused the air between them with substance?

"No, sir, my sister stays in Louisiana," she said. She wondered if he might be an arrogant man, if that was the reason he kept clear of common folk, even if his clothes looked nothing but common.

"You're the youngest one, ain't that right?" he asked, searching for her name.

"They call me Ava." A bird caught her attention and she followed it until it flew off.

"The birds gave my granddaddy our name so I owe them a few favors." She explained, brushing the crumbs off the table into the grass.

A dab of frosting hung from the knife she held in her hand. He reached over the table and ran a finger along the knife in her hand.

"Can you forgive a man for stealing a taste?" he asked.

He placed the lump of white frosting in his mouth and smiled.

"Whipped cream?"

She nodded twice.

A hot, slow moment hung between them until a savannah sparrow, a splash of yellow above its beak, swooped down where the crumbs had fallen and then was joined by a second and third bird. The children, by now, were hopping up and down the church steps.

"Seems to me, Ava Morning, I may or may not be half-cute but there's nothing half about you, is there?" he teased.

"You weren't half disappointed that you didn't figure me in for a slice of cake or half-happy I know whipped cream from butter. You're all the way, huh? A hundred percent Ava."

When the sparrows had flown off, she looked back at him. "You think you have me figured out, but just 'cause you got a nice smile don't mean you know me. You ask a lot a questions but you haven't done a thing with an answer yet."

Real quietly he said, "I'm gonna leave you alone, girl. You're too much for me."

It felt wrong to go but he forced himself, in his worn-out dungarees and his sweat-stained shirt, around the church and down the road. He did not actually think himself above the other people in the town, he just needed to take every precaution necessary to escape the place that had stolen his mother and cheated his father. As he walked away a searing pain over his left eyebrow forced him to close it against the bright sunshine. He had no way of knowing that Ava, through one eye, had just gotten in.

∗

Lewis Bank's drove slowly, trying to avoid the ruts in the rough road. It was nearing spring, snow still blanketed the fields, but an early thaw had turned parts of the unpaved road into mud. He was not accustomed to driving an automobile and he feared getting stuck on the desolate road, although he knew it was not much further, having passed the sign a few miles back.

Detective Hobbs had come the month before. He had asked around for the owner of the old pickup truck, the only vehicle on the reservation whose engine turned over in the cold months. "I am looking for a Lee Smith," the detective had said repeatedly. "I am looking for a man named Lee Smith whose name this truck is registered under."

He was answered by a group of somber faces, a few shrugs. Was there a hint of laughter in a few of the men's eyes? Finally, someone brought grandmother to the door.

She cleared her throat and called out to where the detective stood. "Who do you ask for?"

"Lee Smith. He owns this truck according to my papers."

"I know everyone on this land. There has never been a Lee Smith."

"Well, can you please tell me who owns this truck then?" Detective Hobbs said, stamping his feet to fight off the cold.

Grandmother remained silent. The wrinkles around her eyes were deep; her hair white as the snow under her feet. Chayton stood among the group in the yard, next to the rain barrel that had a thick sheet of ice across the top. Of course he could not hear what the man asked but he could tell by watching the man's face and his grandmother's, that it was some business with the truck. They relied on it for their farm work and to get into the city each month but could anyone beyond their land covet the old rusty thing? He looked again at his grandmother, whose eyes were now closed.

"Who owns it?" she said just when the detective had decided she'd fallen asleep on her feet. "Same as who owns this land. Nobody. We just use it." Then she hugged her coat tighter and turned slowly, disappearing into the house. The others moved off slowly, no one looking back. The detective knew he would get no more answers. Besides, he had a more pressing assignment than this one, so he left a note for Lewis Banks that there was nothing else he could do. On the back of the note he scribbled directions to the reservation.

✶

Lewis swerved to miss a deep rut in the road and felt the car slide toward a low bank of snow. He cut back in the opposite direction and hit the break, forgetting to engage the clutch, causing the engine to die. He counted to five before turning the key to get the car started again. It caught but when he tried to move forward, the wheels spun. He tried again. He was stuck. He put the gear in reverse and tried to rock backwards but the car still wouldn't move. After a few minutes he cut the motor and started walking toward a small group of houses up ahead.

He had tried to let the matter rest after the detective's note. He had paid Hobbs and thought that would be the end of it. But it wasn't. It nagged him. It pestered him as he worked, while he slept, while he listened to Camille describe her day over their evening meal. He needed to see the man who had killed his daughter. He needed the man to see him.

As he got closer, he saw a figure walking toward him. It was a boy with a dog at his side. Lewis stopped, the dog made him hesitate.

The boy called ahead, "Trouble with your car?"

Lewis nodded. He heard the dog growl real low at the young boy's feet and tried not to look down.

"Got stuck. With all the mud and wet snow the wheels just keep spinning. What's your dog's name?"

"Hound," the boy answered. "I guess it could have been dog or hound, but turned out to be Hound." The boy stared at Lewis. He reached down and patted the dog's side. The dog seemed to relax. "We don't get many visitors. You must have made a wrong turn? Come on."

Once the boy turned around, the dog bounded off. Lewis could hear it laboring across the packed snow even after it had disappeared around a house. He heard a door bang. He followed the boy, careful to keep his footing where the snow had turned icy, toward the three small houses set in a semi-circle facing each other. When they rounded the corner of the first house, Lewis found himself just a few strides away from the pickup truck. It was blue. The fender in the back stuck out beyond the rusty body. An empty crate sat in the back amidst the snow.

Lewis stood still. First he heard the quiet of the country around him. The absence of frivolous noise; beeps, rumbles, shouts, whistles. He could hear the wind moving the bare trees above; he could hear his breath. Then he heard a bird call from somewhere far above. Just a quick shrill note that reminded Lewis of his first life, at the foot of the mountain in West Virginia. *How did I get here,* he wondered, *standing on flat, barren land, in front of the truck that killed my child?*

The boy also stopped, watching Lewis Banks staring at the truck. Then he dashed into the only house with smoke coming from its chimney. The other two were smaller, more dilapidated, no bigger in size than the little cabin Lewis had grown up in. A man came out followed by the boy. They waited for Lewis to speak.

"My car is stuck down the road a bit. I'm afraid I'll need some help getting it moving again."

"What made you drive out to begin with?" asked the man. He was thin and his coat had been patched where it had worn through at the elbows.

Lewis paused. "The truck," he nodded at it, "I need to see the person who drives that truck."

Grandmother had been standing in the doorframe listening. The clouds hid the sun's path but it was close to noon and still Chayton was not back from the river.

"Invite him in," she called out. It had been many years since she had seen a black person and never out here. She knew something had happened with the truck, ever since that Hobbs man had been out, but she could not guess what the matter involved.

As Lewis entered the small house, he was surprised to find it crowded with people. Young children played jacks on the floor, two women were at the table and a handful of men gathered around the wood-burning stove, still wrapped in their coats. The room came to a halt, those in it completely surprised by the visitor. Grandmother nodded toward the men, they rose to leave. They had come to visit, share a cup of coffee. They stayed in the cluster of houses on the other side of the glen, a small grove of birch, maple and white pine dividing one side from the other. The stream, where Chayton liked to fish, ran through the glen, the river flowed a mile further. The men left quietly, shooing the children outside with them. One woman disappeared in a back room, the other pulled out a chair from the table for Lewis. The man who had brought Lewis inside took a seat by the stove.

"I have no food to offer you. We are waiting for the fish. But there is coffee," said Grandmother. "Winona, a cup?"

Winona was Grandmother's eldest daughter. Most people called her Rose but her mother liked to call her by the name given to first-born daughters. She set a tin cup of warm coffee in front of Lewis. The man by the stove was now facing the table; he was another of Grandmother's children.

"Thank you," said Lewis.

They waited for him to speak his business. Lewis had not anticipated having trouble explaining himself. He had built up a litany of words meant to wound the person who was responsible for his heartache. He had massaged his anger for months, eager to taste the bile of revenge. Even if his revenge would only be a blast of hard, cruel accusations thrown in the man's face. He had not expected a cold, crowded cabin with no food for the table.

"I have come because something happened. Something with the truck outside," he said in a voice that sent a chill through Grandmother. She stood up abruptly, causing the coffee in Lewis' cup to lurch over the side and splash onto the table. She closed her eyes and held up her hand. She needed to prepare herself for whatever bad news the man was here to deliver. She had already suffered more pain than her heart had room for.

"I remember during our war," she began, "there was a black man who fought on our side. They said he killed women and children hiding in their farmhouses and then bragged about it. But at the trial when he spoke, his voice was so mild that they couldn't believe he'd done it. He wasn't hung. Lincoln pardoned over 200 but he didn't save us all.

No, he didn't save us all." She paused remembering how her father, like Little Crow in the beginning, had spoken against the fighting. But when the first of the violence erupted, the younger men rode it like a wave until the others were in it as deep. That was what had been taken from them, along with everything else, the power of their leaders.

She shook her head back and forth until she could come back to the man in front of her.

"You are still young," she said softly. "But I see there is sadness in your eyes. Sadness too much like mine. If you have come to take my child. If you have come to take another one of my children, I cannot allow it. I cannot lose one more." And not that one, she said to herself, especially not that one.

She knew the only person who drove the truck any far distance from the reservation was Chayton. She knew he went every month to the city. Something must have happened on one of his trips but she had seen nothing of it in Chayton's face, no hint of something gone wrong in the way he moved his body.

"There was an accident," Lewis began, his voice trembling, "involving my daughter. When she stepped off the streetcar the hem of her dress caught on the fender of a passing…" But he could not say the word truck. "She was to be married this spring. I have no other…" He could not continue. He hung his head and wept, his shoulders shaking. Perhaps he had not come for revenge.

A drop of water leaking through the roof splashed into a metal bucket on the floor. Then the door to the house sprung open and Chayton burst in with a string of fish. He stopped abruptly when he saw Lewis. He was surprised to see a stranger but he was so happy to have caught the fish he blurted out, "It took me awhile but I finally got them to bite. I'll clean them out back." Then he sensed the somber mood of the room and studied the faces of his aunt and grandmother before looking back to the man in the chair. Lewis had composed himself and was sitting up tall.

Grandmother walked over to Chayton and put her hand on his arm.

"This is my great grandson. He is the fisherman of the family. He is the one who gets us through the winters. The one who travels in the blue truck to the city each month to collect the things we need. The one who will marry the girl who loves blue beads and one day, tell his children how long we have been here." Then she turned toward Lewis and continued, "Chayton does not hear so well, so face him when you speak Mr...?"

"Mr. Banks. Lewis Banks," he said. Lewis looked at Chayton. Studied his face, looked him square in the eye for a good, long stretch and found he had nothing to say. There was nothing, in the end, that he needed to take from the young man.

Finally, "You better get to cleaning those fish, son. I should be on my way. Well, yes," he remembered, "I'll need some help with my car, it's stuck."

"I'll get a few men," said the uncle by the stove.

"I can help too," Chayton offered. He left the house to put the fish in a snow bank until he could clean them. Grandmother reached her hand out to Lewis.

In her first language, there was no word for sorry so she never used it. She squeezed his hand instead. "She is not your only child. There are others, I'm sure, that need you." She closed her eyes and then after a moment opened them to add, "Chayton will help you with your car. His heart is big like yours. But he does not hear well. Face him when you speak."

Then she went to sit in the chair near the stove and rest. Lewis swallowed hard. The man who killed his daughter did not even know that it had happened. He walked out into the yard. The clouds were still thick and the wind high in the tops of the trees. He did not look at the truck this time. He followed the men to the car, listening to their footsteps against the crusty snow. Listening to the songs of the first birds, chasing away winter.

14

"Can you do me a favor?" Frances asked, as they tumbled out of the Broadway Movie Theater at half-past nine on Saturday night.

"Sure, doll," Joe Mallory replied. To her relief he had not tried to put his arm around her during the show, which now left her feeling obligated to act pleasantly toward him. He's not so bad, she told herself, ordinary or not.

She waited while the crowd dispersed from the mouth of the theater. The audience for the next show had already been let in, shuffling along the sticky floor toward their worn velvet seats. She had spent the past two hours staring at the screen but not hearing a word of what the actors were saying. She raised her eyebrows whenever Joe looked over, hoping to convey her intrigue with the twisting plot when, in fact, she was mulling over how she could find a way to get to Cotton. She felt it urgent to show him the letter she had found that morning. She had only seen him the one time, but she knew where he lived. Tomorrow, Sunday, would need to be spent with her family—there was church and then dinner following their afternoon walk through the park—and yet it wouldn't do to wait for a whole week until next Saturday and the free morning it usually granted.

"Well, what is it?" Joe said.

She decided to forge ahead with her plan, latching onto the wide look on his face as an invitation. "Can you drive me someplace?"

"Sure, I got a little gas," he smiled.

As he pulled his father's car away from the curb, she saw

him glance at his gasoline gauge. "Where to?"

"That-a-way," she pointed. Through some indiscernible place below the car's dashboard a draft of cold air flooded through her nylons and pressed adamantly against her shins. She thought for a moment of how sensible a pair of slacks would prove during a Minnesota winter. In no time they pulled up to Miss Emma's house.

"What's going on, Frances?" Joe squirmed behind the wheel and then, after another glance at the fuel gauge, cut the motor. He had a quarter of a tank left but knew his father would question him if it dropped much lower.

"I'll tell you in a minute. Wait here." She jumped out, running up to the door while nearly slipping on the icy steps.

Miss Emma had fixed Cotton a meal, but he had yet to return home to eat it. She tried her best to be helpful to him, but she knew her actions were insufficient. Still, she prepared his plate every night, whether he ate it or not.

Miss Emma rushed to the door at the sound of the bell. "Who on earth..." she began as she lay eyes on a slender, white woman in a coat with sleeves just a hair too short. "Can I help you?"

Frances explained she was looking for Cotton, said she was a friend of Hazel's and knew Mrs. Banks. "I really need to speak with him," she insisted.

Finally Miss Emma said, "You might find him at the cafe 'round the corner. They stay open late now on Saturdays and sometimes he takes his supper there. Can't say for sure." She paused for a moment, then added, "He don't need no trouble. Keep your fellow with you so nothing looks, well, funny-like."

Back in the car Frances ordered Joe to drive up the block and around the corner. They pulled up into a space directly in front of the cafe. Through the frost-edged windows Cotton could not be seen at any of the tables, but she figured he had to be inside.

"It's the last thing I'll ask," she began. "You've been a real good sport and honest I appreciate it."

"What's gotten into you Frances? What are you messed up in? Are you asking me to go in there? You've got me down in this neighborhood and now you want me to go in some filthy joint and, what, eat dinner with these people?"

She stared at him. Strange the things you don't find out about someone until they get nervous. "No, just stay in the car then and if you can't wait, you're free to leave. I'll figure a way home."

"You're crazy," he yelled as she walked off.

She, too, was nervous as she entered the restaurant. The door rattled in its frame and then banged shut behind her, causing the clamorous room to go still. She stomped her boots on a gritty rug and looked up into a sea of faces. There were at least ten tables, most filled, but no sight of Cotton anywhere.

"Can I help you?" said a waitress, holding a coffee pot in one hand. The restaurant began to murmur again, turning its overt attention away from the stranger who had just come in.

"Yes, I'm looking for someone named Cotton. I was told he might be here. He's tall and rather ..."

"We know Cotton," the waitress said. "Comes in often but not tonight."

"Oh, gosh," Frances muttered. "It's so important that I find him."

The waitress put up her free hand, "I try not to mettle in other people's business. Either way, he's not around tonight."

"Oh, I see." Then she tried again, "It's just that I have something I need to show him." Here she lowered her voice, which seemed to draw in the waitress and a man at the closest table. "Something that belonged to his fiancée."

The waitress looked over at the man. She shrugged one shoulder at him, and then filled his coffee cup. The man, his hair gone entirely gray just in the past few months, wiped his mouth slowly with a napkin before addressing Frances. "Cotton's next door at the pool hall," he said.

She had to go back in the car and plead with Joe Mallory to take her next door. When that didn't work she accused him of being a coward and neglectful to consider allowing her, his date, to enter such an establishment unaccompanied. Cognizant of her culpability in dragging him unknowingly into all of this, she focused on his earlier derogatory remark about the neighborhood to quell her guilt. Finally, because his feet felt frozen and he was not to be called a coward—for it really was a bum right knee that had kept him out of uniform—he agreed to go in.

They stepped into a dim smoky haze thickened by music, the thud of beer bottles against the bar top, the collision of pool balls, the voices of people laughing or arguing. She soon spotted Cotton seated on a stool at the bar and began to make her way toward him. She did not look back to see if Joe would follow.

"Hello," she yelled. Cotton turned toward her, his eyes glossy.

"What gives, man?" said a guy standing next to him, who now placed a hand on his shoulder. "Who is this?"

Joe arrived behind Frances.

"Beats me," Cotton said. Then he sang, "I don't know nobody and nobody knows me. That's the way it's been and the way it's gonna be." He turned back and snatched up his bottle.

"Excuse me. I was hoping I could talk to you. You might not remember me, from the night of the accident," her voice raised above the noise. "But I was there when it happened."

Cotton stared at the brown bottle, rubbing the damp label so that the paper wore away under his thumb. It was too much to turn and look at her.

"My man says he don't know you, lady," said the man behind Cotton. "And he never tells a lie, do you man? Just like George Washington or was that Lincoln? No, no Johnny Appleseed!"

He laughed and patted Cotton on the back as if they were sharing the joke.

She tried again. "My name is Frances and I was there when Hazel…" She wanted to tell him about how it happened. How Hazel had asked her, with such gravity, to find someone named Hollis. And had then closed her eyes. But he would not look at her and it was not right to shout a truth meant to be told delicately.

"Hey," said Cotton's man, louder now, "No disrespect but you ain't getting the message. This don't seem to be the place for the likes of you or your man. It's best you hit the road, ain't that right Cotton?"

Cotton did not respond but Joe began to tug on Frances's elbow. He could not entirely hear what was being said but he noticed they were drawing more stares now than when they had first come in and he didn't like the bold look in the eye of the man standing. It occurred to him, suddenly, that his car was not safe out front. He suffered a surge of dread at the thought of finding the windows smashed or the tires slit.

She shrugged off Joe's hand.

"Please, you don't have to talk to me but you should look at this," she said holding up the letter. "It's something I think Hazel would have wanted you to see."

Cotton felt the fish sandwich he had eaten earlier, and the beer on top of it, burn in his chest. He wanted to emit a loud burp or, better yet, get up and leave.

He remembered this woman. How she had been there when he had turned and walked away carrying Hazel in his arms. Why was she back? What could she possibly know of what Hazel wanted?

She placed the letter in front of him and said, "I think she figured it would help."

Frances turned to leave, finding Joe Mallory's torso blocking her way. She wanted to give a push but instead scooted around him and toward the door. They drove home silently as she tried, but failed, to convince herself to find a way to be nice to him. Four months ago, she would have overlooked his attitude. But tonight as he pulled the car up to the house on Bryant Avenue, she let herself out and slammed the door.

∗

Cotton took the letter and shoved it into his coat pocket. He hadn't noticed, nor had Frances on her way out, Lewis Banks standing off to the side, with a cap now pulled over his gray hair.

Lewis had watched her leave the café and then lowered his head toward his coffee cup. It was not that his hearing was superior to others, he merely relied on it more. He had heard her car door slam, waited for the sound of the engine, then after a few quiet minutes detected the opening of two doors. Both thudded shut. When the door to the pool hall opened he heard the dim but driving beat of the music and then the sound was gone. He left a coin on the table. He was near certain this was the girl Camille had told him all about. He wondered what his wife would say about her now, sneaking around after Cotton with some mysterious letter. Where had it come from and why not show it to Camille this morning? His anger seethed as he stood just inside the noisy hall, watching Cotton refuse Frances any attention. Had he, as her father, not loved Hazel longer than either of these two could even fathom? What did they know of love?

After Frances fled, he waited for Cotton to move. On Saturday nights, Camille urged her husband to go up the street and check on Cotton, for worry helped to displace some of her sorrow. He and Cotton often shared a table at the café. They struggled to find anything new to talk about but often found a game of checkers an easier way to spend an hour. Lately, it was more common for him to remain alone with his coffee while Cotton drifted toward the barstool next door. At first he thought to just wait—the young man would have no more than one or two—but soon realized it was better to go on ahead home, revealing nothing to his wife of their almost son-in-law's new habits. Tonight Lewis had run low on patience.

He slapped Cotton on the back. "C'mon, the party's over," he said with a light voice but a firm hand.

Cotton was not drunk. His thoughts were pliable and his words cowered behind his tongue but he had no trouble getting up from the bar and leaving with Lewis. Outside, the cold felt good against his face. He reached down for a handful of snow and then threw it against the brick wall.

"Do you need coffee?" Lewis asked.

"No, I'm going home."

Lewis hesitated. He felt less angry now that Cotton seemed to be more in control than first appeared. Perhaps the letter was addressed to Cotton and signed by Hazel, and then of course the girl would have felt compelled to deliver it to Cotton instead of Camille. Possibly a sentimental letter that might make the young man's heart lift but could really offer nothing to him or Camille. And maybe getting old was really a lesson in moving over so the young could step in. Hazel was gone, he knew; every day a fresh loss that no letter would change.

"All right, let's go." They walked home silently, bent against the cold. When it was time to part ways, Lewis merely nodded to the goodnight thrown his way.

✳

The thin, folded paper marked the chapter entitled *The Lover,* the chapter Hazel had begun to read and then decided was as good a place as any to hide the letter until after the Friday night with Cotton; until after she was reassured of how he loved her; until after they had chosen a ring and she could be certain there was nothing, nothing of his past that could make his love for her waiver. What could convince her of that, she had wondered as she clasped her gray pocketbook closed and prepared for their meeting at the jewelry shop? His smile, she decided. If she could just see that smile then the message of the letter would soften into a manageable situation that would not alter the life they had planned.

She had boarded the streetcar, ignoring the looks from the white passengers who couldn't hide their curiosity. It was not the atmosphere inside the car, she was used to such situations, which had her stomach in knots, but rather the content of the letter. She would have to tell Cotton, of course, but couldn't she wait awhile? Couldn't she enjoy this special time without it being spoiled? She stood before the door, waiting: her gray dress pressed evenly along the hemline; the small yellow sailboats, bouncing hopefully upon a vast uncertain sea. She ached to see him, to be reassured by the sight of him. She would clasp his hand and lean into him. Surely, it would all work out fine. In due time she would let him know. At just the right moment.

Minutes later, when she found herself crippled by pain and with only a stranger's face looming over her, it was then she abandoned all hope in her plan. She let go of the idea that she would clasp his hand, that she would take refuge in his smile. She relinquished the tender notion of their future together. Instead, she spent her last few moments considering that there was someone else, out there, whom Cotton could love. In fact, who he would come to need. She locked eyes on the face above her and offered, with two words, the map to change direction.

∗

When her baking clientele grew to include a wealthy white family, Ava and her mama began to eat better, inviting over Tula's household regularly. Although she would have preferred to limit her work to only baking, her job included preparing all three meals and ensuring a spotless kitchen. She would not agree to the domestic responsibilities of the rest of the house—for which the family had to hire someone else—so that she could find time during the day to check in on her mother, who had begun to increase the pace at which her chair rocked. Her employers were not willing to insist Ava take full charge of their house, so as not to jeopardize

Monday's coffee cake or Thursday's peach cobbler.

She found time to continue with the cakes, which she enjoyed most. As she prepared each one she began with the thought of how it would look on completion, imagining the folds and crevices of the swirled frosting, and most of all the color of it. She envisioned the varying shades of white that would become only more intriguing when topped with a splash of nasturtium or violet petals. She loved to watch the cake turn from an array of individual ingredients into a singular creation. Mixing the butter and sugar and then adding one egg at a time, whipping the growing batter with her heavy fork, she carried out a long rebuttal to Cotton's parting remarks, so that after a summer of baking she no longer thought she had anything left to say to him.

In autumn, one night as she finished patting the dinner dishes dry with a worn cloth, she asked May why winter had to bring shorter days. *So there's more time for moonlight*, came May's answer. Ava looked out the window to see if the moon had risen yet above the line of trees at the edge of the woods. The bowl in her hand shook as she spotted Cotton coming through the gate.

She called to her mother resting in the back room, grabbed her sweater and slipped out the door. The moonlight now flooding over Cotton made him even more than he had been under the sun. "It's too late for a proper visit," she admonished in a hushed voice.

After a while, as they walked along a path in the woods together, he reached for her hand.

✳

Cotton withdrew the letter from his pocket and placed it on the bedside table. He sat for a moment in the dark. When he was ready to sleep he eased back against his pillow and tucked the quilt up around him. He stuck out an arm and lifted the letter from the table, drawing it to his face only to find any scent it might have once had now gone. He could no longer remember what his old life smelled like. In disappointment he dropped the letter to his chest and closed his eyes. Within moments he was asleep.

The beer combined with the labor of the workweek drove him deep into a slumber out of which came a dream, like a solitary stone in a clear pool of water, of his mother. When he awoke he could recall only a woman standing in a summer dress calling to him from across the dirt road, the sinking sun behind throwing shadow across her face. He understood through the unproven, inexplicable certainty only dreams allow, that she was his mother.

The thought of her clung to the conscious world as he turned to his side and heard the letter rustle underneath him. He sat up throwing the covers off. A soft light by which he could make out the black ink on the paper allowed him to read the letter. When he finished he lifted his chin toward the window, the moon itself could not be seen through the frame but its light shown and mingled with the first sign of day spreading along the edge of the sky. Cotton remained perched on the bed, shivering, as the first arms of the morning sun reached into the room and found him. He then read the letter again, the post-script too faint to read in the half-light of morning.

August 1943

   Dear Hazel Banks,

   There is something about me and Cotton you best know. His daddy told me how to reach you, said you two was about to marry. Cotton never loved me and I can't exactly say I did back. But one night he came knocking on my door. No one can rightly claim I'm the kind to get in trouble but some nights ain't meant for the word no and not just because the moon was bright.

   I know how much he aimed for a new life so it took until now to write this and still I can't bring myself to send it to him direct. I asked the sky if I should tell him and every single cloud came by yes....

III

15

The very first day of spring, by Frances's calculations, came at half past noon on a Thursday. Having postponed her lunch break to purchase some supplies at Woolworth's, she pushed open the double glass doors and emerged into a surprising pool of warm sunshine. She set out delightedly, finding the need to unbutton her coat as she walked along the trickling sidewalks. Frances made an effort, each year, to catch the first sign of spring, the first mild turn in the air, the initial thaw that suggested an end to the monotony of winter. She treasured that first chance to hold her face to the sun. I'll remember this one particularly, she told herself, as she stepped over a puddle of melting snow.

She stopped for coffee filters and a typewriter ribbon, so that on her return to the office she would have something in hand. Neither item was a purchase of necessity. She collected her change from the clerk and hurried from the store, with six long blocks to cover and not much time. The sun bouncing off the top of the parked cars and the mild stream of air against her face urged her to slow down, but she fought it and pushed forward.

When she reached the entrance to the train station she hesitated. She had only taken the train once, when she was sixteen, to Detroit with Ethel to visit their father's family. Walter had issued them on the train and been waiting on the platform when they returned a week later. She had not paid any attention to the details of ticket buying or train scheduling or luggage handling. Now as she stood amidst a scurrying crowd she felt the swirl of anxiety and excitement that accompanied travel. The large clock on the wall showed 12:39. She was not late.

She found a discreet corner and backed against an iron pillar, careful not to lean against the rust. She watched people board the waiting train, leaving their larger items—suitcases, hatboxes, duffle bags, a bulging pillowcase, a cardboard box tied with twine—huddled on the platform for the porter to load. Frances saw a man in uniform carry the parcels toward the train. After nearly a minute she determined, with disappointment, that it was not Lewis Banks. "Oh, well," she said, although no one around noticed.

They had met the day she had returned to the Banks' home with the borrowed book and a few hours to devote to the room upstairs. It had taken a week to finish the book and then she allowed two more to slip past—to give Cotton some time after reading the letter—before returning to Camille. She wanted the contents of the letter to be Cotton's to divulge and yet she felt disloyal for having taken something from the Banks' home, the letter belonging to their daughter, without making mention of it.

Halfway through the shelving of the remaining books, Lewis Banks had ascended the staircase and stood waiting in the hallway for Frances to pause between sentences. On being introduced by Camille, Frances was bothered by the notion that there was something familiar about him. He, on the other hand, found her demeanor much less assertive than he had witnessed the night she had come into the café searching for Cotton. By the time she left the house, an hour and a conversation later, all boxes had been emptied and the books shelved in an orderly fashion. She waved goodbye, relieved by the success of the visit. She had raised the topic of the letter to find they knew all about it. Even with the work done, Frances continued to visit most Saturdays. That was how she knew to be at the station, at the proper time and, to her delight, on the first unofficial day of spring.

The crowd began to thin as departure time neared. A voice bellowed, warning the remaining riders to board and within minutes the train was moving slowly out of the station. When it was gone, the platform was left lonely and hollow, with only a handful of people milling about. The time was 12:46 according to the large clock, whose second hand could now be heard from where Frances stood.

"It won't be long," a young mother assured a child. The two looked anxiously down the tracks, peering well beyond the shelter of the station but as of yet there was no evidence of an approaching train. The girl tugged on her mother's dress, a raggedy teddy bear dangling out of one hand.

Frances glanced over her shoulder and, down near the end of the platform, spotted Cotton who held a cap in his hand, alternating between clenching it and smoothing it out. She imagined calling out and waving to him. This thought was interrupted by a cry from the little girl who had decided to plop down on the hard cement and demand the train's arrival. The girl's reddening face and tangled expression made an abrupt rebound at the sight of a cherry lollipop drawn from the mother's coat pocket. Amused, Frances returned her focus to Cotton to find him staring at the ground under his feet. He spread a hand over his face, letting a finger and thumb press on each temple, then his arm dropped heavily toward his side. She immediately felt intrusive, as if she was spying on him. She had wondered about the complex mix of emotions he must be facing but she had pushed all that away in her eagerness to witness what she felt she had played a small part in. Now she shrank back, horrified by the certainty of her mistake. She should not have taken the information mentioned to her by Camille as a personal invitation to be present for the train's arrival. She did not belong here.

As she turned to flee, the rising sound of the incoming train amplified her self-doubt. She looked one last time toward Cotton but could not spot him among the shifting crowd. She marched toward the exit, hearing the doors open behind her and the train give off a number of hissing sounds. Just as she stepped onto the public pavement the laugh of a child made her pause. Looking back she found only a sea of faces, none of which she recognized. She marched the six blocks back to the office, ignoring the mild day that had demanded so much of her attention earlier. Her cheeks remained flushed long after she was back at her desk filing the receipts for the purchases she knew Mr. Silverman would not need anytime soon.

✳

It had taken Cotton three months to make a decision, despite Miss Emma's urging.

"Don't miss out," she said. "Don't matter what you feel for the mother, don't miss out on your own flesh and blood." It was she who had informed the Banks that there was a child, not that she thought they were ready to hear it but they needed to be told anyway.

Cotton did not respond to her advice. He had been going to work each day, had stopped the Saturday night drinking and returned to his habit of reading, since it occupied his mind more than anything else. Even so, the reality that he had a son seeped like water into the fertile soil of his mind.

"You might like to send for him," she continued. Miss Emma intended to do her best to keep Cotton. "If you don't dwell on the winters, it's better up here."

Cotton looked into his cup of coffee and for the first time wondered if this was really true. He was grateful to have landed a good job that allowed him to send money home to his father and he did prefer being ignored rather than harassed by white people. Of course finding Hazel had made it simple to dismiss the things from his old life of which he was certain he wanted nothing more. Only for his father was it important to stay linked. The sun falling behind the cotton fields, the hole in the floorboard, the church yard on a wedding day, all of these he had positioned behind the solid frame of Hazel so that they could not be glimpsed. He replaced what he had once called home with the Banks' warm kitchen, breakfasts with Miss Emma and bookshelves for Hazel to fill. But that had all changed.

As he continued to stare into his half-empty cup, he permitted the color of the buttercups that grew wild in front of his father's house to steal back into his thoughts. There was much he hated about Sunset, Arkansas, but it had its beauty and it was, nonetheless, what he knew best and the basis from which to compare all other cloudy afternoons, fence posts, doorframes, wind. In Minnesota he did not have a history, good nor bad, to ground him. Without a future with Hazel he was left floating.

Miss Emma handed Cotton his lunch in a paper sack. "I still got that easel when you're ready. Paints may be a little dried up but all the same I got it waiting for you."

One day last summer, she found his sketch of a garden. She lifted the paper out from where it had slid under a cushion on the back porch, sat down on the chair and studied the image. It looked just like the same garden her granny had grown years back and the woman squatting in the broad-rimmed hat had the contented look her granny used to wear. Before she went in the house she had wiped her face dry, then offered Cotton an easel and some paints a tenant had left years back, saying it didn't matter if he was accustomed to using a pencil. She had told him to brush a little color on and see what happens. The easel had been propped in a corner in the front hall for a week before Hazel was killed, then it was moved to a closet.

Cotton started to leave the kitchen with his lunch clutched in one hand. "I don't even know how to draw anymore," he said.

"I know, but you starting to look ready," she called after him as he continued through the house and left out the front door. He walked the three miles to work, feeling drained inside.

✳

"I reckon," Cotton said on a morning in February, three months later.

He woke earlier than the other boarders so he often ate his breakfast with only Miss Emma in the kitchen. It was still dark in the kitchen, with the ceiling light on above. She looked up from the milk bottle she was opening.

"You reckon what?"

"That it's time to see him. He must be near on seven months now. I wonder if she'd consider bringing him up?" he asked.

"Well, you ain't said a word about her. What kind a gal is she? Is she the mothering kind? I been worried sick for that baby since I known he was in this world." She stopped before saying too much. She had already imagined the boy being given over to Cotton to raise and she stepping in like a grandmother. She bit her lip as she waited for a response.

"She's good," he said, remembering all at once how good she had been to him. He had refused it, had pushed it from his mind as he traveled north. When she crept in he had lifted his head to the changing scenery, sang louder along the desolate roadside, chatted more with the men from whom he hitched rides. As he moved through each city he let the signs, bright and bold with thick black words, blot out the feel of her skin and the smell of the sand beneath her. And when he met Hazel he flung any lingering allegiance to the two nights with Ava into the wilderness of a brand new romance.

"It can't hurt to ask," he said finally to Miss Emma.

He sent a letter later that week. Near the bottom he asked if Ava might consider bringing the baby up to see what the north was like. He included enough money for a train ticket but told her to spend it on something else if she decided not to come. After he signed his name he added a line asking if she could go round and see on his daddy. Cotton sealed the letter and sent it off before he could change his mind, then he carried on with his job, his books, his early breakfasts as if it had not been sent.

One cold damp evening Cotton arrived home after a day of unloading heavy crates at the warehouse. He had pulled a muscle in his back halfway through the day and now as he sloughed off his coat and bent to untie his boots he felt the throbbing increase. He thought to just head up to his room and sleep off the ache but heard his name from the kitchen.

"We're in here eating already," Miss Emma called.

"Evening," he said, coming into the warm room. A new fellow from Chicago and Ralph, who had been staying for years, sat at the table.

"You met Virgil yet?" Ralph asked. "Be careful, he's from Chicago. You know, a big city cat. Don't let him catch a hold of you Cotton, straight from the backwoods."

Cotton nodded in Virgil's direction and gingerly took a seat, the smell of the food assuring him of how important it was to eat. A plate was set down.

"You must of come through Chicago on your way up," Ralph said to Cotton. "Now wouldn't that be so?"

Cotton shook his head and Ralph, accustomed to the one-way conversations, turned his attention on the new fellow.

Miss Emma, while the two men competed over the severity of their respective city's weather, came over to Cotton with a basket of corn muffins. As he reached in for one she slid a postcard under the cloth napkin he had yet to spread out on his lap.

"You need a little pack of ice for that back a yours?" she asked. "Let me wrap up some in a towel for you or you won't sleep right tonight."

The postcard was plain, with only his address and a stamp on the front.

"Here's the pack. Take it upstairs to your room where you can rest proper." Miss Emma cleared his plate, expecting Cotton to opt for a private place to look at the postcard that she

had almost resisted reading. But he picked up the card and
flipped it over. When he finished he looked up at her and
flashed one of his genuine, near-buried smiles. It was the first
one in what seemed like ages.

*

On the morning of Ava and the baby's arrival, Cotton felt
conflicted, his stomach knotted. While he had finally decided
to send for his son out of a sense of obligation, he could not
deny the shifty feelings of curiosity and excitement sneaking
up on him as the day approached. Those moments of near
happiness did not last long before guilt clawed at him like
a meat cleaver. He had vowed to Hazel just seven months
earlier, as he carried her slack body in his arms, to love her
memory with the same fervor he had intended to offer her
while alive. He thought he had wholeheartedly grieved her
absence enough to prevent this softening, this fading, which
thoughts of a baby boy seemed to cause.

He struggled through a morning of work and then reminded the foreman that he would be gone for the afternoon,
having worked an extra shift the week before to compensate.
He made it to the station in time to wipe the perspiration
from his brow before finding an inconspicuous spot on the
platform from which to wait. He wanted the train to arrive
immediately so that he would not have to spend the next ten
minutes sorting through his fluctuating thoughts. He hoped
it would be late, allowing him another moment to pull himself together.

It was not until he had Ava's two bags, she holding the baby
tightly, and they edging down the block toward the streetcar
stop that he noticed the spring like quality to the day.

16

Frances packed an overnight bag. It would be warm but she chose a cotton nightgown that went well below the knee. She folded up a sundress, a modest bathing suit, a small bag for toiletries and a clean pair of under garments. She opted for a scarf rather than rollers and pins. It was a cabin, after all, she reasoned. She squeezed in her latest book from Camille Banks and decided she was ready.

On the front porch the air hung heavy, the children's voices in the yard clinging to the damp skin at the nape of her neck. Her mother and father sat on the porch waiting with her. It was early June and the first stretch of sticky weather had arrived. Irene Pearson from the shoe store and her husband Bud, who had recently returned from service, were to come for her at five and then it would take no more than an hour to reach his parent's lake cottage. Frances had never been to someone's summer place before and while she didn't know Bud very well, she figured she could spend most of her time helping Irene with the baby and enjoying a chance to get out of the muggy city. She had been surprised and delighted when Irene phoned a few days earlier to extend an invitation.

The ride was pleasant. A stream of air came in through the lowered windows while Timmy, perched on Frances's lap in the back seat, misnamed each animal they passed. Irene spent most of the ride turned halfway around laughing at her son. Bud was quiet but smiled occasionally, his hand still bandaged where it had been ripped open by a rusty fence in a small village in France.

Frances eyed the open fields with their young crops and

the lush grasses that grew alongside the narrow highway between towns. When they reached Elk River they stopped at
a stand to buy strawberries before driving the last few miles
around the lake and pulling up in front of a small white cabin
with green shutters. The lake glistened, demanding her attention as she stepped out of the car and stood amidst a scant
bed of wild chamomile and yarrow that had popped up in the
sandy driveway.

Bud's parents were warm and gracious, showing Frances
her tiny bedroom with its wide window facing the lake and
her narrow, springy bed topped with a white coverlet. At dinner they tried to draw her into the conversation but she felt,
despite their friendliness, that there was a hill that she needed to climb to be on the same ground. After dinner they sat
on the dock watching the sun drop into the lake. The waves
eased to a light ripple and Frances began to relax. She dipped
her foot into the water to find it cool. Around the rim of the
lake the trees darkened and the dying sun shown against the
glass of the cabin's windows.

"The Friswold's sent word over that you're to stop by later
for a campfire or a sing-along or whatever young people do
these days. Doris and I can stay with Timmy, as long as you
can get the bugger to sleep before you leave," Bud's father was
saying as Frances swished her foot back and forth in the water.

"Oh that'd be lovely," said Irene. "Then Frances can meet
a few people around the lake."

While Irene sung Timmy his third lullaby, Frances sat
in her little room refastening the buckles on her sandals. As
night fell outside her window, a june bug bumped against the
screen two or three times before lifting off. She felt a surge of
excitement that seemed to lodge just below her navel. What
is this, she thought as she moved on foot down the darken-
ing road with Irene and Bud? What is this, in the midst of so
much life that makes one yearn for even more of it? She felt
greedy for something she couldn't put her finger on.

As they walked down the dirt road a patch of trees rose up on the left. On the right, the lake winked between lilac bushes and cottonwoods and the summer cottages wedged between the road and the water. After a short time they came upon a cabin whose yellow light, glowing above the screen door to the delight of the insects, beckoned them in. Bud knocked once and then pulled the handle open. The kitchen was lit but empty. Bud drew three bottles of beer from an icy tub on the floor before they headed toward the sound of voices coming from the lake. Those huddled around the fire pit let out a low roar as the threesome approached, pleased to see Bud who had missed all of last summer. In the commotion Frances found a spot at the end of a log that pointed out toward the water. The lake now was still as glass and seemed to reflect a gleam from the long departed sun. When things settled down, Irene introduced Frances, but the fire, having burned rather low, made it difficult to make out the half-dozen or so faces around the circle.

A woman named Tip asked, "Where you from Frances?"

"Oh, I live in the city," she said quietly. She felt an acute pinch of self-consciousness over her meager background and hoped she wouldn't be pressed for more information.

"Well gee, we all live in the city, kid. This is just where we summer," came a male voice from a dark spot across the way. "What side of town are you from?"

Frances paused for a moment before she answered. An image of her father came to mind. No matter how strapped for money he was or how long of a stretch he'd be without work, she never once sensed he begrudged the house in which they lived. Then she thought of Cotton, Camille and Lewis Banks, the books she had read and even, maybe especially, Hazel. She had, among these strangers around the campfire, almost forgotten how much she had been through over the past year. She looked around the circle, the fire having leapt up from an added log so that the faces were suddenly bright.

"I live on Bryant Avenue North," she finally answered. Tempted to add that she shared a bed with her younger sister, she held her tongue but smiled to herself.

"Frances," Irene exclaimed, "You haven't even gotten the cap off your beer bottle yet!

"Beer!" someone yelled and then there was a roll call for who needed another one, followed by an arduous coin toss, given the dirt and the darkness, to see who should go fetch a handful from the kitchen. In the mean-time a young man came around to where Frances was seated.

"I have a bottle opener," he said, squatting. "Unless you were planning on saving that for tomorrow night."

She looked at him. The light flickered across the smile on his face. His eyes were very brown.

"I hope you don't mind a small town guy who can get away with a bad joke," he said.

"I'm not so sure you got away with it," she answered. "But thank you. I thought everyone here was from the city?"

"Don't believe everything old Fred tells you."

He went back to his spot across from her. A series of small waves from a lone boat creeping past on a three-speed motor broke against the shore around her heart. She looked over her shoulder at the sandy beach leading up to the water's edge. A canoe, face down with a weathered rope tied to the front, tilted on its side. The waves lapped against the part of the boat that remained in the water. Frances imagined a frog slipping under the boat and taking shelter for the night. She turned back to the circle and saw the young man, the bottle opener still in his hand, watching her. She dropped her gaze toward the fire.

Soon she began to enjoy the crowd. Tip, with her bouncy hair and full figure, seemed always at the center of the conversation, casting her comments in someone's direction before reeling a response back in. Frances gathered that, like Bud, Tip's older brother Fred had already served his time in the war, as had the man with the brown eyes. She wondered which of the women were waiting on a husband or boyfriend to return. She remained quiet on her end of the log, preferring to observe the confident, easy swagger of the gang rather than try to keep up with the banter.

"Hogwash," said Fred, still wearing swimming trunks and a terrycloth beach jacket. "Whether the ice was thick the previous winter bears no impact on how well the fish will bite that summer. Such wives tales have long been disproven thanks to superb fishermen like myself and Jack."

Jack smiled, his brown eyes squinting from the smoke's fire that had streamed toward him unpredictably.

"Oh Fred put a cork in it," Tip piped. "You haven't spent a moment with a fishing pole since dad strung a hammock between those two trees over there. Now Jack would be the only one to know how thick the ice was this past year and maybe the only one who has done enough fishing this season to submit a report on it."

"Well Jack doesn't count, he's a local," leveled Fred. This comment brought forth an exaggerated array of cries denouncing its unfairness.

"Now that's out of line," Bud said, "If I didn't know you better Fred, I'd take that comment seriously and have to throw you off the dock on Jack's behalf."

"There'll be no throwing anyone off the dock tonight," Tip stated. "That can be done tomorrow when all the neighbors can watch."

"Tippy, maybe if we drench it, we can finally get that beach jacket off him," Jack finally spoke.

"What's wrong with this fine piece of clothing?" Fred yelped, standing up and smoothing the jacket over his round belly.

"Enough said!" shouted his sister as the group broke out in laughter.

Frances, finding her giggle slightly beyond her control, decided it best to pour the remainder of her beer discreetly into the grass behind her. She placed the empty bottle between her feet as if it might serve as some kind of anchor. When Irene began to yawn she panicked at the thought of the night ending and, moreover, at having to stand up to maneuver on unsteady ground in the dark.

"I should get back Buddy," Irene called after a few minutes. "To check on the baby."

Bud moaned at the possibility of having to turn in so early. "The night is young," he said, sweeping his hand upward.

Frances looked up and was startled by the stars. There seemed a million more than back home. She felt a yearning streak across the purple sky. The group broke into another uproar trying to determine who would walk Irene and Frances back to their cottage so Bud could continue in his merry way.

"Oh for goodness sakes, I'd be happy to do it," said Jack after a minute of group bickering. Fred attempted his own offer but easily relinquished when he was handed another bottle of beer.

Frances and Irene were issued a round of goodnights as they slipped away from the fire. Jack seemed to appear out of nowhere, suddenly walking between them and pointing out the hammock they needed to move clear of and the grade change as they made their way around the cottage. Once on the road, Frances was amazed at how dark but noisy the night was. She was thankful that the insects thick in the woods on her right had formed a wall of sound to keep her from veering into the weedy grass. She only wished the glow of the lamps inside the cabins would stretch their light a little further out toward the uneven, stone-strewn road.

"Must be a new moon tonight," said Frances.

"Sliver," said Jack pointing up. As she looked up her foot stepped into a slight dip where a bicycle had spun its wheels when the dirt was wet. She stumbled and almost fell before both Jack and Irene reached for her.

"We better walk as a team," suggested Irene. "You be in the

middle, since Jack and I know the road better."

They hooked arms and continued. Frances found the yearning sensation that had stayed with her throughout the evening begin to subside within the dark, saturated night. She felt a sense of certainty that she had landed in exactly the right moment. When they reached the cabin, Irene invited Jack for a swim the next day, to which he agreed.

Frances and Jack found each other just as appealing by daylight as they had the night before. They did not need the backdrop of a party around a campfire to find the same things amusing or interesting. Jack harbored none of the pretense she feared she would find among Irene's summer friends. When it was time to talk about packing up the car for the ride back to the city, they had already exchanged addresses.

"Promise to bring her back," Jack said to Irene.

She would return a number of times later that same summer, but first there was someone closer to home that she still needed to meet.

17

Miss Emma had chosen a room facing the back of the house. She decided that morning light would be best for a child. From it one could stand at the window and see over the entire backyard: the garden, the grove of trees off to the right, the gate that hung skewed on its rusty hinges. She had Cotton bring up a rocker the day before his trip to the train station.

That was months ago and still she had yet to adjust to Ava sharing her pots and pans. With Ava in the house she couldn't keep track of the milk in the icebox or the flour in the canister. Every time she turned around Ava was adding something to an already sufficiently prepared meal. To direct the girl's efforts to another room would have been like nudging a kitten away from a patch of winter sunlight, so Miss Emma used the quiet time of early morning to return the utensils to their proper drawers and restack the baking sheets so they fit together in a sequenced manner. If she could start with everything in place, then she could enjoy a sense of command over the forthcoming day, forgetting that once the baby scooted his chubby body across the kitchen's threshold, her hopes, really her urge, for an orderly kitchen would be squashed by the little one's boisterous cry and his mother's inability to sit still in a kitchen.

With her morning cup of coffee in hand, she went out to the back step to look over the garden. Gazing at the herb bed along the border, she decided today the sage needed thinning. And the rabbits seemed to be back at the parsley.

She would have to sprinkle cayenne pepper on the soil and

if that didn't work try a tuft of human hair at the base of each plant. It was a tactic her grandmother swore by but which required some effort to carry out. She would peek around at dinner tonight for a shaggy headed tenant. There weren't many to choose from.

Of course there was still old, nearly bald Ralph who shared a room with a thin man whose first name she never could get straight. Two others had left last month and she hadn't lifted a finger to replace them. While normally word of mouth brought borders her way, she realized with two empty attic rooms and Ava taking up another room, having refused to accept the extra cash Cotton offered for their stay, she should think about posting a sign on the church bulletin board. But she could not bring herself to do so.

She could not, just yet, do anything that might alter what she had found since the baby's arrival. She knew Cotton to be the one who had brought her a burst of sunshine, but his boy had come along to throw open every window in the house. After all the years of boarders making noise and taking up space but never filling the silence, she finally went to bed at night feeling like loneliness had not followed her up the back staircase. And she awoke eager for her turn to hold the little boy on her hip. Her one persistent worry was how long it would last.

From the step she heard someone moving in the kitchen behind her. In a moment she would go in and see about breakfast, but it was Saturday and she wanted another minute of the early morning light.

Cotton was not hungry, anyway. He stood in the center of the kitchen looking out through the door, beyond Miss Emma's seated figure, gazing at the shades of green layered in a thick pattern known as a garden. One ear was half-cocked, as always, for the sound of his son's voice.

He liked to recall the first time he heard it.

✳

The train had arrived on time. He had to wait for most of the passengers to descend before spotting Ava as she came down with the baby asleep in her arms. He did not smile at her and she did not smile back.

"The ride all right?"

"All right," she answered, certain by his first dry question that it had been a mistake to come. At nine months the baby was heavy in her arms but she gave no indication of it.

Cotton looked to the boy but his sleeping face was turned into his mother's coat, so he reached for her bags instead.

"This away out," he nodded in the direction Frances had headed minutes earlier. She was nearly back to her office by now.

"Since we're walking past, I best use it. If it's okay?" Ava said. They were in front of the ladies room.

"Go on ahead," he said. Although he avoided public restrooms, there was no sign barring her from going in. She hesitated.

"Go on now," he said again with a hint of tenderness in his voice that she would lean on over the hard days to come.

"Take this boy for me then," she said, handing over the child. Just before she disappeared into the restroom she added, "I call him Hollis."

The child stirred for a moment in his father's arms, then melted back into slumber. His face now was turned up toward the sky. Cotton studied it while the word Hollis washed over him like a beam of sunshine on the very first day of spring. It was more than how the boy looked; it was the blood rushing through veins and the heart pumping rhythmically, whispering the two syllables of his name. It was the warmth of his son's skin that captured the father's full attention, so that Ava had to place her hand to Cotton's elbow to let him know she had returned.

He gave the baby back and again took up the bags. When they reached the street, the sun shone on the sleeping boy's face.

"We'll take the streetcar," he said casually, as if he had not entirely avoided riding it since the accident. Being midday there were plenty of empty seats. They rode the first ten minutes in silence until Hollis sat up with a jerk, looked hard at his father and uttered his first word, "Duck."

At this, while the car rattled toward their stop, Cotton smiled full and long, something else Ava would need to keep.

✶

Cotton shook himself out of the memory.

"Morning, Miss Emma," he said coming out through the back door.

"A blessed morning it is. The sky is a color I can't fit to name. What have you planned for Sonny today?"

"Depends on his mama," Cotton answered.

"Maybe his mama is waiting for you to say. All three of you could head to the creek before it gets too hot?"

He didn't respond. He walked closer to the edge of the garden and bent down.

"Seems like something's at your parsley again."

"Seems like it."

Cotton stayed in a squat. When he reached out and pinched the lemon thyme the scent clung to his fingers. He told himself it was a good day to visit Lewis and Camille. Just as last Saturday and the one before had been. But he had not been able to do it. They had only met Hollis once and Ava never. He struggled to imagine how to make it work. Make them understand he had not abandoned their daughter in order to claim his son.

Emma sighed and rose up from the stoop.

"You done right, Cotton, bringing them here," she said, as if reading his thoughts. "Don't know how it'll turn out but you made a strong decision and done right by it."

"It doesn't feel so right," he said.

"How so?"

"Hazel," he said her name roughly as if he had to get it out quickly or it wouldn't come at all. "Turned my back on her."

"Son it may seem, just yet, like that's true but I don't believe God makes love something like water in a jar, something you gotta worry about spilling or drinking up. Your son's a lesson in that. Love can just keep coming from every direction. Just because you now love Hollis don't mean you love Hazel less."

Cotton stood to face Miss Emma. The hazy morning floated between them, moving through the small gaps the atoms of the body can't keep out so that her voice became as wet as the garden dew. She added, "Same with Ava... I'm no expert, having shunned most chances at love. But the lack of it in my own life hasn't kept me from seeing signs of it in others. You get more than a jar, Cotton. More than one jar already half empty 'cause it's been knocked over."

"Dadeee," came a cry from behind the screen door and out came a bubbly Hollis squirming about in his mother's arms. Ava greeted Miss Emma and came out to hand the boy to Cotton.

"I can keep him in the kitchen while I fix breakfast but he won't stand not to see you first." Apart from talking to her baby, Ava didn't speak much throughout the day except for sentences like this. Having realized quite early that she had been naive in thinking Cotton had sent for the both of them, she figured silence the best medium to heal the wound of her miscalculation. She intended to soon be fine and clear-sighted enough to decide her next move.

Miss Emma headed into the house, leaving the three of them alone at the garden's edge. Ava went to take Hollis back.

"No, no, no, no, no," the baby protested.

"Seems like he's hollering to stay," said Cotton. "I can keep him."

As she turned to go, he added, "Any chance you'd consider fixing us something special today? My sweet tooth is acting up."

"I'll think on it," she said keeping her back to him. She felt the wings of an insect flutter against her ear as she pulled on the door handle, disappearing inside where the warm flush that spread across her cheeks could not be detected in the muted light.

✳

That same morning Frances sat at the breakfast table with her family. Her mother took off her apron and placed her hands on her hips.

"There," she said, "the basket for Uncle Clive is all put together." She nodded at Ethel, who with school out could not use homework as an excuse. "I'm expecting you to come with us today, young lady." She then turned to Frances. "And it'd be nice if you would join us too, it's been such a long while since you walked up. Seems every Saturday you're as busy as can be."

"Today is the same," Frances began, fingering the buttons on the front of her blouse. "After I help with chores, I'll be busy into the afternoon."

"I know you're near grown dear," said Mary, "but I'd like to know just what takes up your Saturdays. Am I not right, Walter? Being a family under one roof, I think it's something we should know."

"Don't you visit the library most times, Fran?" Walter asked, not really wanting to be part of the conversation. He was hoping later to try fishing with his buddy Earl at Cedar Lake and his mind was mulling over what type of bait to use.

Frances looked from her mother to her father and back to her mother again. She was suddenly very tired of fabricating half-truths about how she spent her time.

"Yes, I do visit the library," she began. "But often I walk all the way past 6th Avenue and visit the Banks' home, you know, Hazel's parents. Her mother seems to enjoy the company and she has shelves full of books she lets me take. It's nearly a full hour one way so the trip tends to use up half the day. Often I stop at the library on the way back to read through some of the books I borrow."

Mary and Walter stared at their daughter. Ethel was still at the table but the other children were already outside.

"I'm sorry I kept it from you, but it's true I am grown," she said. "And there's no real danger in it, honest. People are real friendly, that I pass."

Mary huffed around the house for a while but in the end agreed that Frances was old enough to choose how to spend her Saturdays. She seemed to calm down when Walter suggested he walk along with Frances since he was thinking of fishing over in that direction, give or take a few turns.

When the laundry was hung in the side yard, she set out with her father. The sky had grown overcast, keeping the air mild. She liked cloudy days, when thoughts seemed to hold together better. She realized that it was near time to tell her parents about brown-eyed Jack and her plan to see him again. He had written twice.

*

Ava came into the house, Cotton and Hollis still giggling in the yard, to find Miss Emma pouring eggs into a hot skillet. She paused, wondering what to bake. She spent a good part of most days in the kitchen. She was very efficient, given the boy tugging at her dress. She was uncertain as to whether Cotton was giving Miss Emma something for their stay, so she worked hard trying to help feed the people in the house. Her sense of obligation and her need to be active produced biscuits and meat pies, loaves of bread and an occasional rice pudding but her unhappiness prevented anything fancier and left those who ate her food leaving the table with a thought for a handful of raspberries from the garden or a dose of cream for their evening coffee. This morning she was puzzled over Cotton's request. A fruit tart was too much, perhaps muffins with a spoonful of jam on top or flapjacks with maple syrup.

"I don't need no help this morning child," came Miss

Emma's voice to shatter Ava's thoughts. "I got it, now. You helped me enough all week. Maybe you'd like a little time for yourself. Freshen up some, for Cotton."

Ava was pretty sure she had heard right, only it didn't make sense so she asked May for verification. Her sister seemed confused as well because all Ava could hear was a rise of cicada bugs panicking in the trees above the house. When the insect's shrill wave subsided Miss Emma continued.

"It's gonna take a bit a work and a good deal of patience. Cotton is still struggling from a blow. He may need a little space yet, even so it's time you get to it. Slow at first, most things that last start slow. Now go up and draw you a bath. I know its morning but ain't nothing wrong with a morning bath unless you got something big like a Joe Louis fight coming at night. Ain't that silly how folks will bathe and dress up to sit at home and listen to them fights? Been awhile, with the war now, since we got to hear a good one." She laughed, then added, "Crush these sprigs of lavender in the water but when you're done, scoop them back out or they'll clog my drain."

Ava did not move yet. She needed something more.

"Why today, ma'am? Why all this time passed and now you say something about Cotton to me?"

Miss Emma laughed again. "Why *not* today?" She pointed to the calendar on the wall as she nudged the stiffening eggs with her spatula. "July fourteenth. Good a day as any for an old woman to start giving advice."

Ava spun around to look at the calendar hanging by a nail against the wall.

"Oh, May, can you believe I might could a missed it?" she blurted.

"Missed what and who, good gracious, is May?" asked Miss Emma.

"Today Hollis turns one. I need to make a cake!" she reached for her apron on the hook behind the door.

Ava explained, as she took the last four eggs from the

basket next to Miss Emma, how she fell into the habit of asking her sister May for advice. Then she thought it only right to mention Tula and the rest of her family. She was pouring the batter into three greased and floured cake pans by the time she had finished explaining how her mother had seemed relieved to move down to Tula's house when it came time for Ava and Hollis to leave.

"I think she was tired of looking at them woods."

Miss Emma's scrambled eggs were cold and stiff in the frying pan. Somehow no one had come in the kitchen to eat. At one point, Ralph arrived looking for coffee but they had shooed him out after one cup. Cotton and Hollis had drifted down to the creek. Ava had spoken more in the hour that just passed than she had in the three months since she arrived and her heart was lighter for it.

"You planning to put those pans in now?" Miss Emma asked.

"I was fixin' to. They take a good hour. Then I plan to ice 'em up fancy. Could we spare some raspberries from the bushes out back?"

"Of course. Now put them in and then you get in that bathtub. Don't forget the lavender on the table."

Before Ava left the kitchen she asked one last question.

"I thank you for the encouragement, ma'am. I really do. But he hasn't shown no signs of tenderness but for the baby. Not a thing toward me. What makes you think it's worth trying?"

Miss Emma came over to Ava, placed a hand on the young woman's cheek. "You try for the sake a trying, girl. That's what makes anything worthwhile. The trying itself."

✳

Cotton and the boy came back midmorning, hungry and tired. The cake, not yet frosted, was hidden in the pantry. Ava was whipping the cream. She had thought to add the juice from a few crushed raspberries to turn it pink but she couldn't stand to lose the snow-white color. When she heard them coming up the back she slid a plate over the bowl of just picked berries.

Hollis let out a cry for his mother, who came to him with open arms. Cotton was thrown by the smile on her face. He realized how rarely, as of late, she used it. Standing there babbling with the baby, he took in her clean, summery dress and the color in her cheeks. It seemed as if her hair was combed a different way. He had always liked the smell of lavender and he wondered if the scent was rolling all the way up from the garden.

"You two must be hungry," Ava said and moved to get some breakfast. She set Hollis on the floor. When she stood up, Cotton was still looking at her.

While Cotton napped with his son in the crook of his arm on the sofa in the front room, the sky turned overcast. Miss Emma, dusting the furniture on the main floor, peered out the window. Her garden needed rain but the color of the clouds didn't suggest they'd oblige. She knew Ava was in the kitchen, shaving chocolate over the raspberries that topped the cake. She figured the child would need less than an hour more of sleep. She went out the front door and walked down the block until she reached the Banks' home. She rang the door without hesitation. Camille answered.

"I came by to invite you to a birthday celebration, Camille. The baby turns one today and we baked him a cake. We'd love for you and Lewis to come by after lunch."

Camille let out a small puff of air at the thought of her neighbor's request.

"Thank you, Emma but Lewis is working. Won't be back till Tuesday."

The two women stared at each other. Camille had not finished suffering the daily loss of her daughter. She had displaced so many of her own aspirations onto Hazel that she now found herself staring at a vast landscape of emptiness that she feared neither she nor her husband had the ability to fill. While she needed him, there were periods of silence between them that she could not see across. She had found no way to avoid the small disaster that occurred inside her each morning, leveling any chance for a good day. Why visits from Frances helped, she couldn't exactly say except that there was some connection between the young woman and the kind of memories Camille needed to keep Hazel near. Frances was upstairs now, browsing through the books.

"I have a guest," she added.

"All the better. Way I see it, the more the merrier for a birthday party," Emma grinned, she was well aware of Frances's visits. "I'll see you then? In about an hour, that way Hollis will be up from his nap."

Camille closed the door. She had met the baby once before, by accident. Cotton had passed by as she was arriving home from the market. She had not asked the baby's name. Now the name Hollis rolled across her chest like far-away thunder. She mounted the stairs with as much steam as she could generate, finding her breath jagged by the time she entered the room where Frances sat in a reading chair. She waited for her heart rate to slow. The curtains hung motionless beside the open windows. The clouds had thickened but not darkened and the space between things and other things, people and other people had narrowed. Camille could feel the weight of Frances's thoughts hanging above the open book, could hear the swish of Miss Emma's dress moving across the street, could smell the almond oil she had, long ago, rubbed in Hazel's hair before parting it.

She had nearly forgotten there was such a scent.

"Are you okay, Mrs. Banks?" Frances asked rising from the chair.

Camille stared at Frances. "How in the world," she began, thinking out loud, "did you end up here and my Hazel nowhere to be found?"

Frances froze. Her mind raced backward searching for specific examples of Mrs. Banks directly inviting her to the house. Had she read the signs wrong? Had she invented the relationship she had thought well established up until a moment ago?

Camille continued, "No one would believe me if I told them my daughter is dead and instead I have a fill-in every other Saturday. Someone who is nothing like her and yet has become my only friend." She walked across to the window and stood with her back to Frances.

"That is a sad comment on my ability to make friends, isn't it, given you and I are not really friends are we Frances? We could not really be friends when you can never really know what it is like to be me and, to be fair, I can't imagine being you. Yet I appreciate you coming, really I do. It reminds me that I did have a daughter, after all you were there to see her take her last breath."

A silence crept about the room and tangled in both women's hair.

Camille spoke. "I want to ask you something. Hollis is the one Hazel asked you to find, right? Cotton's little boy's name is Hollis?"

"Yes, it is. He's the one."

Camille had stuffed the name under the lid where she kept things too confusing for her tired mind to figure out. She had once believed in dreams and then had come to realize they didn't matter either. Yet, now as she turned back to face Frances, she thought it might help to make sense of it all.

"It's the boy's first birthday today. You and I have been invited to join them for cake." She looked beyond the conversation into the possibility of the coming hour. Then, returning her gaze to Frances she added, "Why was it so important to Hazel when that baby was some other woman's child?"

Frances smiled at Camille. Suddenly, she was not deterred by Camille's attempt to diminish their friendship. She smiled at the thought of Hazel seizing, in the very last moment, a chance to do something good and unselfish. To take a name, written in pencil at the bottom of a letter, and utter it out loud.

"Hazel would want us to go meet Hollis, wouldn't she, Mrs. Banks?"

And to Frances, Camille's face softened a little.

18

A small table with one wobbly leg had been pulled out onto the back porch. Cotton fussed with it trying to make it steady enough to hold the cake. The porch was small and cluttered; the floorboards had once been painted gray.

Ava stood with the cake in her arms waiting. She frowned, "This won't do."

"Give me a minute," he said looking for something to wedge under the uncooperative leg.

"It ain't the table," she said, "it's the space. Bring it down into the yard so we can move about and catch some air. Be closer to the flowers."

Cotton looked up at Ava. Until now she had not made one demand that he could remember.

"If you don't mind," she added.

He positioned the table near the peonies, drooping with their heavy white blossoms, where later in the summer sunflowers would stand with beaming faces and become, as she would admit to him, Ava's favorites. Despite the unevenness of the thick grass, the table did not rock under his hand when he felt for it. Ava had gone back into the house with the cake, remembering she hadn't found a candle yet. Cotton waited, listening to the women and the baby clattering about in the kitchen. He did not want to think about his earlier conversation with Miss Emma but he could feel that it had already worked its way in.

As he stood in the yard, a light mist brushed against his bare arms. He looked up hoping the rain would hold off. He thought of Hazel and realized he had gone all morning without her on his mind. He waited for the pang of guilt to stab at him. Again the mist brushed his arm. He ran his hand along the table, hoping it hadn't become too wet for the cake. The wood was dry under his fingers.

The screen door flew open and the noisy group tumbled down the steps and into the yard, old Ralph followed with a stack of plates. The cake was lit and Hollis was screeching in delight or horror, Cotton couldn't tell which. Miss Emma recommended blowing the candle out before the baby dove head first into the raspberries. Singing went better, Hollis smiling sheepishly in his daddy's arms.

"You cut it, Cotton," Ava said handing him the cake knife. As he took it from her hand he was flooded with the memory of their first meeting, in a yard with a table and a white cake. She smiled as well, as if she too were remembering. For a moment their smiles met.

While the forks were being set on each round plate with a sound that made the baby say "ding" and then giggle, Frances Lang opened the squeaky gate and made her way through the yard, toward the most beautiful cake she had ever seen. At that same moment, Walter Lang was floating on a lake in a fishing boat with no bait on his hook and Lewis Banks was walking through a dining car trying to imagine what small gift he might bring home for his wife. Camille was standing in the middle of her daughter's empty bedroom wondering, despite an effort not to, what was happening three houses away. Chayton was walking under a young white pine.

Hollis had heard the gate click and watched the young woman as she approached. When she reached the lavender bush sprawling half-way into the path, he pointed an index finger covered in white frosting and called out "duck" to which the group of people—some happy, the rest working toward it—laughed so hard the sound floated up and over and out into the world where anyone who needed it might make it their own.

Acknowledgements

I begin with those who came before me to create the path on which this story could travel. Those I knew, those I read of and those I had to imagine. Thank you to my parents and grandparents, cousins, aunts and uncles. I credit my father, Robert Knaeble, who instilled in me an obligation to the truth and to my mother, Bernice Knaeble, who painted for me the world captured in these pages. To my eleven siblings (Alan, Stephan, Bernadette, Joseph, Catherine, John, Jeanne, Elizabeth, Andrew, Martin and Jennifer) and their spouses and children, from whom I learned how to belong. To my great Aunts Helen and Esther who we would walk down to visit, sometimes dragging our feet, to a house that the characters in my book came to live in. To my husband's family, Robert Williams, Gloria and Bill Jones and Juanita Haskins, whose stories provided my Southern characters with a place to grow up in.

Thanks to those I met along the way that didn't think the idea of being a writer was entirely foolish. Dara Goldberg, Jane Whitlock, Barb Bolstorff, Rebecca Lunna, Luis Player-Delgado, Homer Magpiong, Rita Faye Knaeble, Josine Peters, Mary Hartnett, and especially to Jovelyn Richards who insisted and insisted and insisted. A bow to my husband, Keith Williams, for his unwavering support and that sense of confidence that has been rubbing off on me since the day we met. And of course, to my son Mason and my daughter Carmen, whose wit and charm and optimism rises up like laughter in a garden on a summer day.

Lastly, thank you Forty Press for finding Hollis, especially Nick Dimassis, my editor, who used his vision to move the story and yet allow my voice to tell it. I am especially grateful to Catherine Knaeble for reading the manuscript in its many stages and for her creativity, along with Katie Knaeble, in turning out a fabulous cover.

CPSIA information can be obtained at www.ICGtesting.com
Printed in the USA
LVOW10s1536021014

406990LV00009B/1198/P